# KIOWA TEXAS

By Troy J. Cauley

To Bill, wherever he is.

# ACKNOWLEDGMENTS

Many thanks to Helen Haught Fanick, Michael Simpson, and Peter Gael for their assistance.

# Foreword

A couple of years ago, I had a little book called *Texas Town and other Verses* published. I should hate to have to prove in open court that it was a book of poetry. Mostly it was a group of thumbnail sketches of people and a few incidents in their lives. Whatever it was, it has met with some degree of approval by readers and numerous appeals for an expansion of the characters and their lives. That's what this book is supposed to be, definitely in prose this time. The names I have used have been picked at random.

Terry Cauley
Austin, Texas
June 26, 1986

## The Rubber Box

Kiowa, Texas, is my hometown. It wasn't very big when I was a boy, and it still isn't. I don't reckon it ever will be.

But my family was big; five boys, five girls, plus my father and mother, of course. We weren't exactly poor, but we certainly weren't rich. I was next to the oldest, and I wanted to go to the University of Texas and become a lawyer, like Colonel Brandon, so I could make speeches and run for public office. It was clear to me that if I were going to go to college, I would have to pay for it mostly myself.

So during my last year in high school and the first year after I graduated, I worked in Mr. London Brown's drugstore and saved all the money I made. During those two years I learned more about people — good, bad and middling— than I ever had before or ever have since.

For example: when I started working there, Mr. Brown had a deal fixed up in the back room so that a man could come in and drop fifty cents in a box and take out a package of rubbers, and nobody but him would know anything about it.

We called it the Rubber Box. It was right next to the door to the men's room, so a man could go back there for a legitimate purpose and transact the other business, too. Lots of men, especially good church members, were embarrassed to come in and ask for a package of rubbers, especially if there were any other people in the store at the time, so this deal saved their feelings.

It worked all right for a long time — even Jesse

James Weaver was honest about it— but then one summer something went wrong. Mr. Brown began to notice that a lot more packages were going out than half dollars were coming in. He felt mighty hurt about it. He didn't like losing the half dollars, of course; but worse than that, he was hurt, he said, by the men's dishonesty. They had abused his trust in them.

"Maybe it's Gabe Hopson that's doing it," I said.

Gabe Hopson was lowdown, trashy, trifling, and otherwise, good for nothing. He swigged chock-beer, stole chickens, beat his wife, and shot craps. He fished on Sunday, swore at his mules, starved his children, and kept bad company. He stayed up late at night, slept late in the morning, and didn't believe in sending missionaries to the heathens. He bet on baseball games, played poker in the livery stable, and promoted dogfights. He was pigeon-toed, knock-kneed, and bow-legged; his ears flopped; his eyes didn't gee; and his feet weren't mates. Also, he didn't have any well-to-do kinfolks, so it was considered safe to accuse him of anything that went wrong.

"It could be," Mr. Brown said; "but I don't remember ever seeing him come back here — not more than a time or two anyway."

"That's right," I said; "I haven't seen him in here in a long time. Maybe he's sending somebody to do it for him?"

"Maybe," Mr. Brown said; "but I'm afraid not. I'm afraid it's somebody else, and I'm afraid I know who it is. We'll have to find out."

So for the next several days and nights he had me hide behind the Coca Cola barrels in the back room and watch the Rubber Box. It was pretty tedious for me. It was too dark to read, and I got tired just sitting there and doing nothing. Especially in the mornings. Men don't seem to be interested in rubbers or anything like that in the mornings. The Rubber Box didn't have any customers at all until late in the evening or at night. But I had to sit there and watch all day.

I made up word games to pass the time. I would see how many towns in Texas I could think of that started with *A* — like Austin, Amarillo, Abilene, and so on. When I couldn't think of anymore *A's*, I went on the *B's*—like Brownsville, Beaumont, Belton and so forth. It wasn't exactly a rollicking sort of thing, but it did help to pass the time.

When I got tired of that, I made up a list of all the men I could remember seeing go into the back room in recent weeks. I had to write the names pretty much in the dark, and sometimes they sort of overlapped on the paper. Then when one of these men came in and didn't rob the Rubber Box, I would cross his name off the list. That way I began to narrow things down considerably.

But the next Saturday afternoon the big detective act went all to pieces. The drug-store up front was full of customers, and Mr. Brown called me to come help wait on them. He may have been hurt about the Rubber Box, but he would have been hurt any amount worse by losing a sale because a customer didn't get waited on in time. So I had to leave the back room for about half an hour.

But even while I was waiting on customers, I tried to keep an eye on the door to the back room. During that half hour or so, I saw six people go back there:

Mr. Benjamin Franklin Eden, president of the First National Bank of Kiowa, pillar of the community, head of a family of grown-up sons and daughters, and with respect to money, as tight as the bark on a tree.

Brother Ben Flowers, the Baptist preacher, the rouser of revivals, the upholder of morals, the scourge of the sinful, who had put nineteen young people out of the church for dancing and sixteen others for smoking and drinking.

Tom Junior Throckmorton, son of the merchant prince of Kiowa, who, to the despair of his mother, ran around with Bobby Lorene Pressley, a tough girl from the wrong side of the creek.

A travelling salesman from the Waco Drug Company who called on Mr. Brown every week. He knew every waitress between Waco and Lubbock and any number of farmers' daughters to boot. He had been shot at by a good many of those same farmers, but none of them had hit him yet. He could stomp the starter on his Dodge roadster and get going in a hurry.

Albert Bright, who had gone to school for twelve years and made it through the fourth grade, definitely feebleminded, ordinarily friendly and harmless, but known on occasion to chase little girls.

Trafalgar Brown, son of Mr. London Brown, and thus heir to the drug-store, who was home for the summer from prep school, and doing quite well with the poorer class of girls in town, and maybe with some of the better class, too.

As soon as I had a minute, I hurried back to the Rubber Box and investigated. A dozen packages were gone, and there were no half dollars to take their place.

I told Mr. Brown about the loss and told him whom I had seen go back there.

He looked very sad.

"I was afraid he's been taking them," he said.

"Who?" I said.

"Never mind," he said. "We'll quit using the Rubber Box. Anybody who wants rubbers will have to ask for them — and *pay* for them."

I never could figure out whom he meant. Maybe you can.

# Hot Weather

It was August. The weather was hot and business was poor. The drug-store was in the middle of the block on the north side of the square, facing south. That meant that the midday sun bounced off the pavement right through the front door.

Dr. Chock McCollum, the dentist, stopped by the drugstore on his way back to his office after lunch. He stood under the fan in front of the soda fountain and looked at the sidewalk.

"I'll bet," he said, "it's hot enough on that sidewalk to fry an egg."

Bill and I didn't disagree with him.

After he was gone, Bill said, "Let's see about this."

He took an egg from the soda fountain, broke it into a glass, and took it out and poured it on what looked like the hottest part of the sidewalk, and when nobody was looking, he went back to the prescription case and got a beaker full of carbolic acid, brought it out, and poured it on the egg. The acid cooked the protein in the egg and made it look just as if it had been fried in grease right there on the sidewalk.

I struck a match and held it under the bulb of the big Cardui thermometer that hung by the side of the front door. The flame ran the mercury up from 105° to 150°.

If you think we couldn't have done all of these things without somebody's seeing us, you just don't know Kiowa in August. We didn't have to wait more than fifteen minutes until somebody came along.

It was Mr. Caspar Greenleaf, a man who had just moved his family to Texas from Illinois. He stopped and looked at the egg on the sidewalk. You could tell that he didn't approve of it.

"What's that?" he asked.

"It's a fried egg," Bill said.

"What's it doing there?"

"We put it there to see if the sidewalk was hot enough to fry it; and it did."

Mr. Greenleaf took out his handkerchief and wiped his face.

"How hot *is* it, anyway?" he asked.

"I don't know," I said, "but there's a thermometer there by the door. You can see what it says."

He walked over and looked at it. The reading had dropped to about 145°, but even that seemed to impress him. He sort of moaned and wiped his face again.

By that time several other men and boys had gathered round to see what was going on. When they asked, Bill pointed to the egg and the thermometer.

"I'll bet that's a new record," Jim Ashmore said. "We ought to send it in to Ripley's."

"I've seen it a lot hotter than this," Ethan Wetzel said. He could always top anything. "Just wait till the last week of August."

"Will it be hotter than this?" Mr. Greenleaf asked.

"It'll be a lot hotter than this," Ethan said.

Mr. Greenleaf looked at the egg again and then at the thermometer. He was a big fat man with a pale blond complexion. I thought he swayed a little as he looked at the thermometer again.

All of a sudden, he keeled over in a dead faint. Bailey McDonald tried to catch him, but Bailey was a little man, and Mr. Greenleafs carcass went through his arms like a six-shooter bullet through tissue paper. The hardest part of it was that Mr. Greenleafs head struck the sharp corner of the steel doorframe. It cut a big gash, and the blood ran down all over his face and neck.

The men picked him up — Bill and I helped — and tried to carry him up to Dr. Clinton's office, which was upstairs over the drugstore. But we had a hard time of it. The stairs were narrow and steep, and halfway up there was a right-angle turn. And Mr. Greenleaf was heavy and sweaty. It was hard to get a good hold on him. He was always slipping out of our hands and bumping on the steps. And, we had to sort of drag him around that corner. I reckon there must have been a square foot or two of skin scraped off his back by the time we got him onto Dr. Clinton's couch.

The doctor worked on him a long time, sent me down to the soda fountain to get some chipped ice, and patched up the skinned places. About sundown they took him home and put him in bed, and he stayed there till after the first norther that fall.

When he was able to be up and about again, he went to see Andy Haywood, the low-downest shyster in Kiowa County, and arranged to file suit against Mr. Brown. He alleged that Bill and I had made false pretenses concerning the weather, which had led to grievous bodily harm and suffering on his part, also loss of employment and other damages. He was suing for $10,000, which in Kiowa, Texas, in the Year of Our Lord 1922, was roughly the equivalent of $3,000,000 now.

When Mr. Brown got notice of the suit, he told Bill and me that if he lost it we would have to work for nothing long enough to pay back whatever he lost. In view of what he was paying us, we figured that would take two or three normal lifetimes; so we decided we had better do something about the matter.

Colonel Brandon was an old-time Texian, a Confederate veteran, and probably the best criminal lawyer west of Fort Worth. His office was up on the third floor of the Masonic Temple. We climbed the stairs, sat on his horse-hair sofa, and told him about our case.

He listened carefully and politely and asked one

question. "You say he came here from Illinois?"

"Yes, that's right. He still gives us checks on a bank in a town in Illinois."

"Just like a damn-yankee," the Colonel said. "Boys, don't worry another worry. If this thing comes up in court, I'll chase those two out of town."

I felt a lot better, and I'm sure Bill did, too.

"What about a retainer fee?" I said, using a big word I had heard my father use.

"I think a dollar would be about right," Colonel Brandon said. "Fifty cents apiece for you boys."

We paid him cash and went back to the drug-store.

The case came up for trial in the October term of District Court. Colonel Brandon didn't even listen while Andy Haywood was orating about how Bill and I had imposed upon a simple, unsuspecting stranger who had lately come to make his home among us by making false and misleading statements concerning the heat and related matters. Andy put his heart into it, as well as his up-creek tabernacle voice; and it sounded mighty bad for Bill and me. I think we would have settled for a suspended sentence if the judge had given us a chance at that point.

When Andy finally got through, Colonel Brandon stood up and called Mr. Greenleaf as his first witness.

"Mr. Greenleaf," he said, "I take it that you are not familiar with our Texas summers?"

"No, thank God, this was my first one."

"Where did you reside before coming here?"

"In a civilized country — Blaine County, Illinois."

"I take it then that your forefathers did not participate in the Battle of the Alamo?"

"I didn't have four fathers—I had only one and I never heard of the Alamo."

"You never heard of the Alamo?"

"Wait a minute — maybe I have. Was that the old

church that didn't have a back door?"

Colonel Brandon disdained to answer the question. Instead he turned to another part of the evidence.

"What was your family's position with respect to the late unpleasantness sometimes called the Civil War but properly designated as the War Between the States?"

"I'm proud to say my father fought to save the Union from the Slaveholders' Rebellion."

"Of what political party are you a member, Mr. Greenleaf?"

"I have voted the straight Republican ticket all my life."

"Your Honor," Colonel Brandon said, "I move the dismissal of the case. I will show my magnanimity by not pressing charges against the plaintiff for attacking my client's building with his obviously misguided head."

"Case dismissed," the judge said.

Poor Mr. Greenleaf had one misfortune after another. He lost his job at the brick plant because he was away from work so much; his wife developed a case of the blind-staggers; his daughter ran off with a drummer from Dallas; and his son got caught bootlegging.

That winter the Greenleafs moved back to Illinois. I don't reckon they ever did learn to like Texas.

# The Rain-Maker

It had been dry for a long time. It hadn't rained since some time way back in the spring. In fact, it hadn't rained any to speak of in about two years.

Lots of people came into the drug-store and stood under the electric fan and drank the free ice water I gave them from the soda fountain and complained about the drought.

"The preachers ought to take it up." Obidiah Robertson said. "The preachers ought to call a meeting at one of the churches and have all the people come and stay all day and fast and pray for rain. The preachers ought to do it."

"You reckon God ain't heard about the drought?" Uncle Clint Barrow said. "Seem like as long as it has been going on he'd have heard about it."

"The people ought to pray," Obidiah said, "they ought to call on the Lord."

"Don't you reckon the Lord knows his business?" Uncle Clint said.

"The people ought to humble theirselves in the sight of the Lord," Obidiah said, "They ought to get down on their knees and beg the Lord for rain."

"If I was God," Uncle Clint said, "and they come around me whinin' for rain, I'd slap 'em down. Hell, they knowed this was a dry country when they come here."

"You don't understand God," Obidiah said, "You don't know how his mind works."

"If he don't know we need rain, he's mighty behind the times," Uncle Clint said, "and if he does know it and ain't done nothin' about it, I ain't aimin' to ask him to. I can be just as independent as he can."

"It wouldn't do any good if you did ask him," Obidiah said, "because you ain't a true believer. You don't believe in your heart."

"Let's see some of you true believers give it a try," Uncle Clint said. "Why don't you jog the Lord's memory? You're as true a believer as ever I seen."

Obidiah was a Free Will Martinite Baptist. He lived on a farm about three miles out east of town. His boys worked the farm and he stood around town and argued religion with the rest of the loafers. He was one of the best free ice-water customers I ever had at the drugstore.

"I'm glad to hear you say that, Uncle Clint," Obidiah said. "I try to be a true believer and the Lord has given me grace to be one."

"I couldn't agree with you more," Uncle Clint said. "When it comes to believin' in the Lord, you're the genuwine *article*."

"Thank you, Uncle Clint," Obidiah said.

"Now, Obidiah, will the Lord answer a good man's prayer?" Uncle Clint said.

"The Lord will always answer the prayers of a man who comes to him in the right spirit," Obidiah said.

"That's fine," Uncle Clint said. "Now, Obidiah, I want you to pray for rain. You're a good man and I know you'll go to the Lord in the right spirit, and anybody can tell that this country needs rain. I've been in this county since 1854, and I ain't ever seen it need rain worse than it does now."

"We do need a good rain, and that's a fact," Obidiah said.

"That's right," Uncle Clint said, "so I want you to start prayin' for rain right now, and I'll bet the whole two thousand acres in that place of mine down on Kiowa Creek against your hundred and sixty that you can't get a drop of rain in the next week. I say a week because I think that ought to be long enough for you to get in touch with the Lord and for him to do something about the matter if he wants to. I don't want to rush him."

Obidiah was flabbergasted. "That's a blasphemy," he said. "I won't have nothin' to do with such talk. The very idea of bettin' on what the Lord will do or won't do! I won't have nothin' to do with the whole idea!"

"I thought you'd crawfish," Uncle Clint said. "You holy birds always crawfish when the chips are down."

"I'm not crawfishin'," Obidiah said. "I don't gamble in any shape, form, or fashion. It's agin all religion to gamble."

"All right then," Uncle Clint said, " we'll leave off the bettin' part. You just plain pray for rain because a lot of good, hardworkin', God-fearin' people here in West Texas need rain, and there won't be no bet on how it comes out. See how many inches of moisture you can get that way."

"I won't do that neither," Obidiah said. "The Bible says 'Thou shalt not tempt the Lord thy God' and that's just the kind of thing it's talkin' about when it says that. If the Lord wanted it to rain, he'd make it rain all right without me temptin' him about it. I won't do nothin' of the kind."

"I thought you'd crawfish on that one, too." Uncle Clint said. "You and the Lord had better get together on this thing if you want intelligent people to believe in you."

"I won't stay around here and hear the Lord insulted anymore," Obidiah said. "I won't listen to no more blasphemy." He walked off down the sidewalk toward home. Some of the people who had been listening laughed at him because they thought Uncle Clint had got the best of the argument.

You might think that would have been the end of it but it wasn't. The funny thing is that in less than an hour after Obidiah left it began to cloud up over in the northwest. A big black cloud formed over Reservoir Hill, and by four o'clock it was thundering and the lightning was flashing all over the place. A few minutes later a hard wind struck, and it wasn't any time after that till drops of rain as big as half dollars were coming down. It rained harder and harder for the next two hours. It poured down like I'd never seen it before in my life. It got so dark we had to turn on the lights in the drug-store at five o'clock. It rained so hard, I was pretty nearly scared.

And then about six o'clock it slackened up a little and settled down to a good steady rain that lasted all night. At seven o'clock the next morning when I came to work I looked at the Government rain gauge out on the courthouse lawn, and it showed eight and five-tenths inches of rain. That's what I'd call a rain.

That afternoon pretty much the same bunch of loafers was in the drug-store that had been there the day before. Obidiah Robertson walked in as proud as Joe Bailey. He stood as straight up as he could and shook his finger at Uncle Clint.

"Uncle Clint," he said, "let this be a lesson to you and don't ever again doubt the power of prayer. The Lord has answered your blasphemy."

"The hell you say," Uncle Clint said. "Who prayed for this rain?"

"I did," Obidiah said.

"You left here yesterday evenin' sayin' you wouldn't have a thing to do with prayin' for rain. You said it would be temptin' the Lord, " Uncle Clint said.

"The Lord changed my mind," Obidiah said. "While I was walkin' home from here, the Lord spoke to me. He said 'Obidiah, go ahead and pray for rain; I'm with you.' So I dropped down on my knees right there under that big cottonwood tree on the north side of road, at the corner of my place, and prayed for rain. And I reckon you folks seen for yourself how the Lord answered my humble prayer."

"Was that before the cloud come up or after?" Uncle Clint said.

"I didn't notice," Obidiah said.

"Obidiah," Uncle Clint said, "you're more kinds of a liar than a honest man could shake a stick at."

"Every word is the gospel truth," Obidiah said.

And right there is where we have to leave it. Lots of people agreed with Uncle Clint that Obidiah was a bare-faced liar, and lots of other people believed that Obidiah really had brought on the rain.

You can still start a good argument by just dropping into the drug-store some afternoon and mentioning the matter. I've done it lots of times when things were sort of dull.

Anyway, Ben Rickets took up a collection for Obidiah because the rain had helped the whole county so much. Lots of people gave a quarter or a half a dollar just because they appreciated the rain so much whether Obidiah had anything to do with it or not.

The collection amounted to over fifty dollars, and Obidiah used the money to run a pipe from his windmill out to his garden, so his boys could water the vegetables during the long dry spells we're always having in West Texas.

# Big Six

One morning in October I was coming to work a little before seven o'clock. Just as I was passing the XL Livery Stable, I saw Big Six come out of her house next door and start over toward the livery stable.

Big Six was a bad woman. Her real name was Mrs. Lula Watson, but she didn't have a husband anymore. He had quit her when she started running around with other men. But she did have three children; and the oldest one, Bonnie Lue, was beginning to grow up. She was about fifteen years old and had a figure that bulged in just the right paces.

The livery stable wasn't a livery stable anymore. Joe Tilden kept his service cars there. Joe had a son, Chigger Tilden, about eighteen or nineteen years old, who drove one of the service cars. He thought he was the red-hot stuff. He ran around with traveling salesmen whenever he got the chance, and he talked a mighty good game of poker and chasing women.

That morning when I saw Big Six headed for the livery stable, I remembered that the night before Chigger Tilden had brought Bonnie Lue Watson into the drug-store and bought her a chocolate milkshake. While she was drinking it, he came back to the prescription case and bought a package of rubbers. So I figured that Big Six was probably looking for Chigger, and I thought it might be interesting when she found him. So I stood in the front door of the livery stable and watched.

Chigger was asleep on a cot. He had his clothes on except he was barefooted. Joe Tilden was sitting at a table drinking a saucer of coffee and there were two other service-car drivers sitting with him. Big Six didn't pay any attention to them. She walked across the big room toward the cot where Chigger was. She had on high-heeled bedroom slippers and the heels clicked on the floor like dice. She grabbed Chigger by his hair and jerked him out of bed. He squawked like a game rooster. She stood him up on his feet and slapped him back onto the cot. Then she jerked him up again and slapped him on the other side of his face. Chigger really woke up after that one and rolled over behind the cot next to the wall. When Big Six tried to reach him there, he rolled under the cot. His bare feet stuck out from under the end of the cot and Big Six stomped his toes with her high heels. He yelled like the boogers had him and jerked his feet under the cot. She knocked her shin on the side of the cot and swore like two mule skinners.

By that time the noise had attracted a whole bunch of men. They came crowding into the livery stable to see what the riot was about, and pretty soon they were all rooting for Big Six. She didn't pay any attention to them though. She concentrated on Chigger. She found a broom and prodded him with the end of the handle. He yelped but he didn't come out. She picked up a handful of old spark plugs and threw them at him but most of them went wild. Then she picked up a handful of horse manure from one of the old stalls and threw that at him. I guess it must have got in his eyes because he caterwauled worse than he had before.

All the time she was trying to get him out from under the cot, she was cussing him.

"I'll learn you to take my daughter out and keep her out all night, you sorry bastard," she said. "You leave that girl alone or I'll cut you from one end to the other!"

She called him more bad names in more different ways than I could think up in a year. She had talent for that kind of thing.

Joe Tilden said, "Chigger, don't let that old bitch talk to you that way!"

"I ain't listenin' to her," Chigger said.

Then Big Six saw the kettle the men had been using to heat water for making coffee. She grabbed it off the stove and started toward the cot with it.

"Look out, Chigger," Joe yelled, "she's going to scald you."

Chigger scrambled out from under  the cot and lit out for the front door. Big Six came right after him with the kettle. Her kimona came open all down the front and she didn't have on anything under it. I guess it was her working clothes. Her hair came halfway up to her navel and her breasts were as big as watermelons. I reckon she was all female. She was so hellbent on scalding Chigger she didn't even notice that her kimona had come open. He got out the front door and she chased him down the block, yelling and swearing as loud as she could rip. She was gaining on him, and all of the men were rooting for her.

"I'll give you fifty dollars if you'll catch him and castrate him right here," Logan Barnes yelled.

"Get that fifty out of your pocket," Big Six yelled back.

But at the corner one of her slippers came off and she stumped her toe on a bump in the sidewalk and fell down. The kettle of water splashed all over her. I reckon it wasn't hot enough to really burn her much, but it was plenty wet. When she fell down her kimona flew over head. She was a sorry looking sight.

Chigger got clean away and stayed gone for six months.

Up till Big Six fell down, all the spectators had been on her side; but when she fell down, they all started laughing at her. Which just goes to show how fickle public favor can be.

Big Six got up and wrapped her wet kimona around herself. She tried to push her hair into place, but it was wet and she couldn't do anything with it. When she saw all those men laughing at her, I reckon she was the maddest woman history has ever recorded, as Colonel Brandon would say. She went into her house and slammed the door.

Altogether it was one of the biggest and best shows Kiowa ever had, and it's a shame that it happened so early in the morning when there weren't more people out to see it.

I went on to the drug-store and opened up and swept out. I forgot about Big Six and Chigger pretty soon because I found I had another problem on my hands. Poor old Dr. Clinton was high as a kite that morning. I'll have to tell you a little about him so you'll understand.

Dr. Clinton was a good doctor. He had the biggest practice in Kiowa County. All the women swore by him. They always wanted him when they were going to have a baby. He had delivered thousands of babies and none of them in a hospital. His delivery room was usually the front bedroom in a farmhouse, with a wound-up sheet looped over the foot of the bed for the woman to pull on when the pains came, and neighbor women standing around giving him advice, and flies buzzing in through the open windows. And he didn't lose many babies or many mothers, either.

When he got back to the drug-store after a baby case, he always wrote four prescriptions, always the same four: one for a boric acid solution to wash the baby's eyes, one for an ointment to put on the baby's navel, one for a mild laxative, and one for an antiseptic douche for the mother. I have filled those four prescriptions hundreds of times — sometimes at night when I was so sleepy I could hardly read the labels on the bottles I got the things out of.

Dr. Clinton drove himself day and night. He never

refused to go to see anybody that called him any time whether they ever paid him or not, and lots of them never did. He drove his Model T roadster over the worst roads in the county, and there were some plenty bad ones in those days. And when the roads got too muddy to get a car over them at all, as they sometimes did in the fall and winter, he would ride horseback. He had a big, black stallion, and he rode him like a cowhand.

But there was a mighty sad thing about Dr. Clinton. He took dope. He had started some years before. He would come in from a baby case somewhere way out in the country in the middle of the night, tired and cold and jumpy, and find that he couldn't go to sleep. After an hour or two of twisting and turning in bed with his fat wife, he would open his case and take a little tablet of morphine. Pretty soon it got him and he couldn't stop. He went to New Orleans once and took the cure but it didn't last long. In a little while he was back on the stuff again.

It got to where his own allowance as a licensed physician wasn't enough to satisfy him. Then he would write prescriptions for narcotics for his patients, pretend to deliver them, and use the stuff himself. And one night when he was desperate, he broke in the back window of the drug-store, pried open the narcotics case behind the prescription counter, and stole several packages of morphine, heroin, and codeine. Mr. Brown had to report the loss to the narcotics officers, and it wasn't any time till they found out who did it.

Dr. Clinton was in real trouble that time, but Mr. Brown managed to get him off. He went and took the cure again, but it didn't do any more good than it had before. He got worse and worse — got to where he drank paregoric and anything else he could get hold of. He would forget where he'd left his car and where he was supposed to go. Naturally his practice suffered a good deal, but he was still a good doctor when he wasn't high.

I had a sty on my eye once, and he insisted that I let him lance it. He was plenty high, and I could see his lancet shaking up and down in front of my eye like a flag in the wind.

I was scared to death he would jab it into my eye and put it out, but he didn't. He lanced that sty neatly in spite of the fact that to him I must have looked like I had two heads. He never thought of charging me for anything he did for me.

And I tried to tell people that he was still all right, and I helped him with his calls as much as I could.

On the morning of the Big Six explosion, I could tell as soon as Dr. Clinton came into the drug-store that he had been on a bender the night before and that I would have to watch him all day. He didn't get any calls that morning, but just after I got back from lunch the telephone started ringing like a fire alarm. I answered it, and it was Bonnie Lue Watson. She was screaming. She wanted Dr. Clinton to come quick because her mother had poisoned herself.

I ran up to Dr. Clinton's office to get him.

"Come on, Doctor," I said. "Old Big Six has poisoned herself."

"My goodness," he said, "why did she do that?"

"She stumped her toe this morning and fell down and everybody laughed at her," I said. "I guess it hurt her feelings."

"She oughtn't to take it that hard," he said.

"Come on," I said, "You've got to go down and do something for her right away."

"Do they know what she took?" he said.

"I don't know," I said, "it was probably some of those antiseptic tablets she keeps for her customers."

"Bichloride of mercury?" he said.

"That's right," I said.

"I better take a stomach pump," he said.

I helped him gather up his tools and got him downstairs and into his car.

"Where does she live?" he said.

"You know where she lives," I said, "Right around there next door to the old livery stable."

"I don't quite remember," he said.

I realized I would have to go with him if he was going to get there any time soon.

"I'll drive you down there," I said.

"That'll be fine, " he said.

I drove down to the house and we went in. Bonnie Lue met us at the front door.

"What happened?" Dr. Clinton said.

"She had a run-in with Chigger Tilden this morning," Bonnie Lue said, "and then she came home and started drinking that white mule she keeps under her bed. She kept on drinking and after a while she got a crying jag. I didn't pay much attention to her, because she had left me locked in the kitchen and I didn't want her to know I had crawled out the window. And then a little while ago she started screaming that she was burning up on the inside. I went in and she told me she'd swallowed poison and then I called you."

"Do you know what she took?" Dr. Clinton said.

"The bottle is still in there," Bonnie Lue said.

We went into the bedroom. Big Six was lying on the bed writhing and twisting and heaving and howling bloody murder. She still had on the kimona and it was still open all down the front and she still wasn't paying any attention to it. But I didn't like to look at her now.

"Shouldn't you put some clothes on her?" I said to Bonnie Lue.

"Half of the men in Kiowa have already seen her this

way." she said, "It won't hurt for you two to see her too."

Dr. Clinton looked at the bottle.

"It was bichloride of mercury," he said. "I'll give her an antidote and then we'll pump her stomach out."

He mixed up something in a glass of water and made her drink it, and then he began to get the stomach pump ready. Pumping a person's stomach out is about the messiest job I know of, especially when the person has been drinking corn whiskey and gulping bichloride of mercury tablets. We worked with her for over an hour and finally got her pretty well cleaned out and quieted down.

"Can you do something for me while the doctor is finishing with her?" Bonnie Lue said.

"What do you want me to do?" I said.

"Come in here and I'll show you," she said.

She went into the kitchen and faced the wall and hiked her dress up and pulled her panties down. Her bottom was covered with welts and bruises.

"Mom beat hell out of me with a hairbrush this morning," she said. "I want you to put something on them places. They hurt."

"You mean you want me to rub something on those abrasions?" I said.

"Those what?" she said.

"Those cuts and bruises," I said.

"That's right," she said.

"Couldn't you do it?" I said.

"I can't see back there," she said.

"I don't have anything to rub on them," I said.

"Get something out of the doctor's satchel," she said.

She leaned across the kitchen table, and I decided this was as good a time as any to start practicing medicine. I went in and got a tube of Zinc oxide ointment out of Dr. Clinton's bag and came back and started rubbing it on Bonnie Lue's bottom. It was sort of exciting and I had a hard time keeping my mind on what I was doing. Her hips were firm and muscular. One time my hand slipped and my fingers went where they weren't supposed to.

"Never mind rubbing *that*," Bonnie Lue said; "I ain't sore *there*."

"Excuse me," I said, "my hand slipped."

"Yeh, I know how it is," she said. "Ever since I can remember some man has been trying to let his hand slip in there."

I used the whole tube of ointment. A fly lit on her left hip and slipped off and broke its neck. I may have overdone it a little.

"Thanks," she said, "it feels better already."

She stood up and pulled her panties up.

"I'll pay you for this some time when you can get a night off from the drug-store," she said.

"I can't take pay for it," I said, "it's against the law to take pay for practicing medicine when you don't have a license."

"The hell it is," she said. "Then I'll just make you a present of something."

Dr. Clinton was through with Big Six by that time, so we went back to the drug-store.

"Will she get well, Doctor?" I said.

"Yes, she'll be all right in a few days," he said.

And sure enough she was. She not only got well — she reformed. She quit her profession cold and got a job in the laundry. She wouldn't let men come in her house; and one night when a drunk tried to come in after she'd told him to stay out, she called the sheriff and had him arrested.

She sent her little boy up to Smith's barbershop and had his hair cut and then sent him and the younger daughter to Sunday School at the Pentecostal Church.

In the spring when the Pentecostal people had their big revival, she got converted and joined the church and testified publicly about what the Lord had done for her.

"I used to drink corn liquor, glory to God," she said. "I don't do it anymore, glory to God. It's nasty, glory to God. I'm saved, glory to God, bless his Holy Name."

She didn't say what else she used to do besides drinking corn liquor, but people got the idea; Reverend Raines, the Pentecostal preacher, said her conversion was a miracle. I thought so, too, when I remembered how she chased Chigger Tilden with that kettle of hot water.

The next summer a carnival come to town; and when it left, Bonnie Lue left with it. She had run off with the barker for the hula-hula show.

That was the end of Big Six's reformation. She got drunk and didn't show up at the laundry for three days, so they fired her. By the end of the week word had gotten around that she was open for business at the same old stand. The boys who went down for the reopening reported it was just as good as ever or maybe even a little better because of the rest and recuperation.

# The Sick Mule

Dr. Wilbarger was the veterinarian. He stayed around the drug-store like Dr. Blaine and Dr. Clinton did. His veterinary practice was sort of going down hill because everybody was beginning to use automobiles instead of horses, so he had developed several sidelines.

He used his new Ford for a service car part of the time, fitting professional calls and passenger transportation together whenever he could.

And he dabbled in politics. He was a candidate for the state legislature one year and would have been elected if it hadn't been such a hot summer. He just couldn't get out from under the electric fan in front of the soda fountain long enough to do much campaigning. He was always thinking of running for County Judge, but he never did get around to it. He used to get me to write campaign speeches for him, but I never did get to hear him deliver one of them.

He was also a part-time preacher. He didn't belong to any particular denomination that I ever knew of. I reckon he practiced free enterprise in the field of religion.

And then he was a money lender. He was as tight as Big Six's waistband, so he still had ninety cents out of the first dollar he ever made. Also he had inherited some money from his father. So if you could give him a first mortgage on a hundred and sixty acre farm, four good names on the note, and a character reference from your preacher, he would lend you five hundred dollars at ten percent interest, deducted in advance. He didn't love a dime a bit better than he did his own right eye.

But he had his good points, too, and I always liked him well enough. Besides I had an idea that I was going to have to borrow some money from him before I got through law school, so I tried to stay on his good side.

One night just before it was time for the drug-store to close, he came by and asked me to go on a call with him. Luke Johnson, a farmer out east of town, had a sick mule, and he had called Dr. Wilbarger to come out. The doctor didn't like to drive by himself at night, especially when there was a chance of getting stuck in the sand, so he wanted me to go along with him.

"Sure, doctor," I said "I'll go with you as soon as it's time to close up."

"I'll wait for you," he said.

Luke Johnson lived out in the sandy land about ten miles east of town. He had a wife and twelve children. I think they were the most backward people I've ever known. They had come to Kiowa County from Arkansas — up in the Ozarks — a few years before. They lived almost like animals. I knew them pretty well because their farm was close to my father's cotton gin, and I had visited in that neighborhood during the summers while I was growing up.

The oldest daughter, Effie, was about my age. She was red-headed and freckled-faced, but she was built by a mighty good pattern. She would come into the drug-store and buy Freckle-Eater Cream and Jockey Club perfume with her cotton-picking money, so Bill and I had both gotten pretty well acquainted with her. Bill said if you'd just put a tow sack over her head she'd be one of the prettiest girls you ever saw.

The night Dr. Wilbarger and I went out there, Luke had a lantern out in the pasture where the sick mule was. There was a pretty good moon so we could see our way to walk out to where he was.

"What seems to be wrong, Luke?" Dr. Wilbarger said.

"I don't know, Doc," Luke said. "This jughead took

sick about the middle of the evenin'. He's been down for two or three hours now, and I can't get him up."

"I'll examine him," the doctor said. He took the lantern and began looking at the mule, punching and prodding and feeling around over him and using a lot of technical words to impress Luke.

"This mule has locked bowels." he said when he got through.

"Think of that," Luke said.

"I'll need some drugs that I don't have with me," the doctor said. "Cary, I guess you'll have to drive back to town and make up a prescription for me and bring it back out. And you'd better hurry; this mule is in a critical condition.

"Yessir," I said. I didn't 'specially like the idea of being up so late, but I acted like I didn't mind.

The doctor sat down on a stump, and I held the lantern while he wrote out the prescription. Then I took it and started back to the car where he'd parked it by Luke's barn.

When I got close to the barn, I thought I heard somebody talking. I went around toward the car, and I definitely heard somebody giggle. And it was a girl. You can always tell a girl from a boy when it comes to giggling. I stopped and listened. I heard a girl say, "Go ahead and speak to him."

And then another girl said, "Ain't that you, Cary?"

I recognized Effie Johnson's voice.

"Yes, it is," I said. "Where are you?"

"We're in here in the crib," she said.

"What're you doing in there?" I said.

"We're sleepin' in here," she said. "Pinky Rock is in here with me. She's stayin' all night with me. We didn't want to sleep in the same room in the house with the boys, so we're sleepin' out here."

Pinky giggled to let me know that she was really

there.

"How did you know who I was?" I said.

"We saw you come out with Dr. Wilbarger while ago," Effie said.

"I see," I said.

"You ain't seen nothin' yet," she said. "Why don't you come in and see how we got our bed fixed?"

"I'd like to," I said, "but I've got to drive back to town and get some medicine for Dr. Wilbarger. He's in a hurry."

"What's he need medicine for?" Pinky said. "Ain't he all right?" And then they both giggled their heads off.

"He wants it for the mule," I said.

"What's wrong with the mule?" Pinky said.

"I don't know," I said.

"You mean you're going to drive back to town in Dr. Wilbarger's car by yourself?" Effie said.

"That's right," I said.

"Why don't you take us with you?" she said.

I thought she was kidding. "I'll be glad to have you," I said. "Come on and get in."

She wasn't kidding. They piled out of the barn door and ran over and climbed into the front seat of the car before I could say Jim Ferguson right quick.

"I like to ride in a car," Effie said, "'specially at night with a old, good-lookin' boy."

"I do too," Pinky said.

"Glad to have you," I said. "You don't think you'll get cold?"

They were barefooted and had on cotton nightgowns.

"If we get cold, you'll have to warm us up," Effie said.

She was sitting in the middle next to me.

"I'll do the best I can," I said.

"I'll help if I have to," she said.

I started the car and drove out onto the road. Effie

pushed her leg against mine.

"Be careful," I said: "I have to drive this thing."

"If you have trouble drivin', you can stop," she said.

"I would stop if I wasn't in a hurry to get that medicine," I said.

"What do you care what happens to that old mule?" she said. "He don't belong to you."

"I can't let the doctor down," I said.

"He's down like a snake already," she said and they both had another bad spell of giggling.

The conversation went about like that all the way to town.

It was nearly twelve o'clock when we got back to town and the square was practically deserted, but I didn't want to take any chance of being seen with those two wenches, so I drove around to the alley back of the drug-store and stopped.

"You-all wait here a minute while I go around to the front and unlock," I said. "I can't unlock the back door from the outside."

"We'll be waitin' for you," Effie said.

I walked around to the front and came through the drug-store and opened the back door. The car was empty and I heard somebody coming down the alley. It was Cats Kidman, the night watchman. I wondered where in the world the girls had gone.

"Hello, Cats," I said.

"Is that you, Cary?" he said. "I wondered what was going on back here."

"Nothing," I said; "I just came in to fill a prescription for Dr. Wilbarger."

"How did you happen to park back here?" he said.

"I'm dodging my creditors," I said. "I owe lots of people money."

"The hell you do," he said.

"Ask 'em if you don't believe it," I said.

"There's something funny about this," he said as he started on up the alley.

"I couldn't agree with you more," I said.

"What's that?" he said.

"Nothing," I said.

After he was gone, Effie and Pinky came crawling out from behind a pile of empty packing cases. They had the giggles in a bad way, and I was afraid Cats would hear them and come back.

"Shhhhh," I said.

They giggled worse.

"We heard somebody comin' so we hid out," Effie said.

"That's fine," I said, "now come on in here right quick before he comes back."

They came in and went into the prescription case with me. This was the first time I had seen them in the light. It was disturbing. Effie stuck out in front up at the top and Pinky stuck out behind down at the bottom. Those thin cotton nightgowns didn't cover them very well. And I was afraid somebody would see the light and want to come in. There's always somebody wanting to come into a drug-store.

So I was nervous to begin with when I started making up that prescription. And the girls didn't help a bit as I went along. Effie stood right behind me and tried to look over my shoulder to see what I was doing. She rubbed against my back while I was trying to weigh the things on the little scales. Pinky sat on the high stool with her knees crossed. She didn't have on any pants, of course. I got jitterier and jitterier as time went on.

I checked off the various ingredients as I added them into the mixture and tried to answer Effie's questions about them. When I was nearly through, I noticed there was an ingredient up near the top that I hadn't checked. But I didn't think I had skipped anything as I came down the list. Probably I had put it in but simply failed to check it off. I got to wondering. I knew enough about the ingredients to know that the one I hadn't checked was the most important part of the prescription. It was a powerful purgative. Dr. Wilbarger was depending on it to get the mule back into working order. Without it, the prescription wouldn't do the job at all. I went back and put it in.

I finished mixing the things and got the girls back into the car. Then I had to bar the back door from the inside, go out the front door, and walk around to the back. It all took time but they were safely in the car when I got there. I wouldn't have been surprised if they'd climbed a tree.

The drive back out to Luke's place was something of a trial. The girls had decided I was a hopeless sissy so they felt safe in egging me on as much as they liked. They made a game out of it. Effie looped her legs over mine and tried to sit in my lap. Pinky propped her feet up on the dash and let the wind do what it would with her nightie. It did a good deal.

When we got out of town, Effie had a new thought.

"Stop a minute," she said; "I've got to wee-wee."

"We haven't got time," I said, "that mule may be dying by now."

"If you don't stop and let me out," she said, "I'll wet on your lap."

I decided I'd better let her out. I pulled over to the side of the road. She and Pinky got out.

"I'm afraid of the dark," Effie said. "You'll have to come with me."

"The dark won't hurt you," I said, "It's the same dark you've been in lots of times before."

"If you don't come with me, I'll do it in the car," she said.

I got out. She caught hold of my hand and led me around back of the car.

"You'll have to hold my hand while I do it," she said, "so the boogers won't get me."

I held her hand and she squatted on the other side of me. If somebody had come along in a car just then and seen me standing there holding those two bitches' hands while they wee-weed, I would have died dead on the spot. Fortunately, nobody came along. I got them back in the car and started again.

"I'll pay you two back for all this one of these nights," I said.

"I don't think I'll hold my breath till you do," Effie said.

**No table of contents entries found.**"You weren't gone so long," he said.

"I felt like I was," I said.

"We'll give this suffering animal a big dose of this right away," he said.

Luke and I helped him and we got a whale of a dose down the mule's throat.

"That's all we can do now," the doctor said. "I'm sure the patient will get action from that very shortly. We'll be going now, Luke, and you can let me know in the morning how he's getting along."

"I'll let you know, Doc," Luke said, "and I thank both of you for all you've done tonight."

"You're welcome," I said.

Dr. Wilbarger and I drove back to town and I finally got home and to bed. I dreamed about being chased by Hereford heifers in heat all night.

The next morning Luke Johnson came into the drugstore.

"Well, Luke," Dr. Wilbarger said, "how did the medicine work?"

"Just fine, Doc, just fine," Luke said, "That mule's

bowels moved once before he died and twice afterward."

I turned sort of sick. I had missed all those good chances and still killed the mule.

## Thursday Night

Every Thursday night Mr. Brown went to the Knights of Pythias lodge meeting, so I had charge of the drug-store all by myself. That meant that something interesting happened practically every Thursday night.

For one thing, I always did a big rubber business on Thursday night. Most men didn't like to come in and buy rubbers while Mr. Brown was there. Especially the Baptist men didn't like to. You see, Mr. Brown taught the Adult Men's Bible Class at the Baptist Sunday School, so it didn't seem right for Baptist men to come in and buy rubbers from him. At the same time, they didn't want to buy them from his competitor, Mr. Martin, who was a Methodist. So they waited till he went to the lodge on Thursday night and then came in and bought them from me.

Mr. Brown was always very refined about the rubber business. He didn't like to have items like "Merry Widows — .50" on his books; so he always had Bill and me write "Cigars — .50" when we made a charge sale like that. It was a good system in most ways. Men got to where they would simply come in and ask for fifty cents' worth of cigars, and we would know what they meant, and it saved some of them a lot of embarrassment. But the system had its drawbacks, too. One time we sent Mr. Tracy Willis his monthly bill with "Cigars — .50" on it. It turned out that Mrs. Willis always paid all of the bills in the Willis household. She was a little on the tight side, so she went over each bill with a fine-tooth comb before she paid it. When she came across that "Cigars —.50" on the bill, she went straight up. She came marching into the drug-store waving the bill and foaming at the mouth.

"Look here," she said to me, "you have charged

Tracy with fifty cents' worth of cigars and he never smoked a cigar in his life. Why do you try to rob honest people by charging them with stuff they don't buy? It's an outrage—I'm going over to the District Attorney's office and file suit. I won't be treated this way!"

"Mrs. Willis," I said, "I don't make out the bills. Mr. Brown makes out the bills. You'll have to see him about that."

I knew what had happened, but I thought Mr. Brown ought to have to do the explaining since he was responsible for the system.

She went back to the office and jumped on Mr. Brown.

"What do you mean charging Tracy with fifty cents' worth of cigars when he has never smoked one of the filthy things in his life?" she said.

Mr. Brown turned red as a beet and had a bad coughing spell. He simply couldn't tell Mrs. Willis that those cigars were really Merry Widows. He blew his nose twice and finally managed to say something.

"Mrs. Willis, I didn't sell Tracy those cigars, so I don't know about them. He bought them from Cary, the boy up there at the soda fountain. You'll have to ask him about them."

She came sailing back up to me.

"Mr. Brown says you're the one that charged those cigars to Tracy. I want to know the meaning of it right now!"

I got sort of rattled. I didn't know what to say.

"Yes'm, I reckon I did," I said.

"Tracy never smokes," she said. "What would he want with cigars?"

"Maybe he wanted them for somebody else," I said.

"Did you ask him who he wanted them for?" she said.

"No'm." I said, "When a man comes in here and asks

for fifty cents' worth of cigars, we just assume he wants them for his wife."

"For his *wife*," she screamed. "Are you insinuating that I smoke cigars?"

I saw I was getting into a tight spot, but I didn't know how to get out.

"You see, Mrs. Willis," I said, "these were a special kind of cigars."

"I don't smoke *any* kind of cigars," she said.

I was getting mixed up worse and worse.

"No'm," I said, "you don't smoke this kind of cigars, you use them for another purpose."

"Maybe you're trying to tell me that I used those cigars to keep from having moths," she said.

"No, Mrs. Willis, you use them to keep from having babies," I said.

"*What?*" she said.

"Nothing," I said.

And then I had an idea.

"Mrs. Willis," I said, "why don't you go home and ask your husband about those cigars? I'm sure he can explain them to you so you'll understand."

She must have gotten the idea about that time, for she went galloping out of the drug-store like she was in a hurry. I don't think she ever came in again as long as I worked there.

Mr. Brown bawled me out pretty bad about what I said to her, but I still don't see how I could have handled the situation any better. After all, he had a chance to explain it to her, and he didn't do it.

But to get back to Thursday night. I 'specially remember four Thursday nights in a row that first year I worked at the drug-store. On the first of these four Thursday nights, Mr. John Barker came in. He was a big ranchman from out west of town.

"Cary," he said, "one of my best cowhands went

down to Fort Worth last week and got a dose of claps. He wants me to bring him a bottle of H.G.C."

"I can sell you that stuff, Mr. Barker," I said, "But it won't do him a speck of good. What he needs to do is to go to a doctor and get treated properly. These patent medicines for gonorrhea are all hokum. We oughtn't to be allowed to sell them."

"He hasn't got time to go to a doctor; he has to work," Mr. Barker said.

"Couldn't you let him off from work for a few days?" I said. "He oughtn't to be riding a horse in that condition anyway."

"He wouldn't go to a doctor even if I let him off from work," Mr. Barker said, "You know how these ignorant cowhands are. You better just let me have that bottle of H.G.C."

"All right," I said, "but it won't do him any good." I started to wrap up the bottle, but then I had another thought.

"Maybe I could tell Dr. Clinton about your hired hand and get him to prescribe for him," I said.

"Do you think that would work?" he said.

"It might," I said. "How long has it been since he got infected?"

"Four days ago tonight," he said.

"When did the discharge begin?" I said.

"Yesterday morning," he said.

"Mr. Barker," I said, "you'd better just go on upstairs and let Dr. Clinton examine you and do this thing right."

"Don't you go telling people I've got the claps," he yelped, "It would ruin me."

"I'm not telling anybody but you," I said; "and I felt sure you knew it already. And Dr. Clinton won't tell anybody either. A doctor will never tell anything like that."

"You give me that bottle of H.G.C. and keep your

mouth shut about this," he said.

"Yessir," I said and finished wrapping up the bottle.

The next Thursday night Dem Witt came in. Dem was a funny sort of fellow. His mother had kind of spoiled him. His father had died when Dem was a baby, and his mother had tried to shield him from the cruel world. Her husband had left her a lot money, so she had done a pretty thorough job of shielding Dem. She had had a separate toilet built for him at school. Some people said she did this so the other boys wouldn't see him when he sat down to pee.

Dem's full name was Demarest Lafayette Witt, but naturally people called him Dem for short. The trouble was that when you said Dem Witt it sounded like you were saying dimwit. His mother expressly forbade people to call him Dem, but it was a law that was mighty hard to enforce. Even when some people said Demarest Witt, they really meant dimwit, so it was a problem that kind of defied solution, as Colonel Brandon would say. And probably the worst trouble of all was that Dem Witt really was sort of dimwitted regardless of what you called him, and his mother with all her money couldn't do a thing in the world about that.

He was about twenty years old, but I don't think he had ever been out at night by himself—I mean without his mother. So I was surprised to see him come into the drugstore that Thursday night. He sidled back to the prescription counter where I was and looked all round the store to be sure there wasn't anybody else there.

"Cary," he said in a sort of stage whisper, "I'm going down to Big Six's tonight."

"It's being done this season," I said. "What do you want me to do about it — pray for you?"

"I've heard about a disease," he said. "Isn't there something that prevents disease?"

"You mean a rubber?" I said.

"I guess that's it," he said. "How does it work?"

"You put it on and wear it, of course," I said. "Don't you even know that?"

"I'm afraid I haven't had much experience with that kind of thing," he said.

I gave him the general idea and he paid me fifty cents cash money and went on out.

The next Thursday night was the really big night of the four I mentioned. Mr. Brown had hardly gotten out the front door on his way to the lodge meeting when Tom Junior Throckmorton and Bobby Lorene Pressley came in. I realized that they had been sitting in Tom Junior's Model T out in front waiting for Mr. Brown to leave.

It was easy to see that Tom Junior was scared to death. He was nervous and pale. But Bobby Lorene looked like she was pretty well in control of the situation.

"What can I do for you-all?" I said.

Tom Junior started to say something but he couldn't quite make it. His mouth moved but nothing came out. He tried again but it went the same way. Bobby Lorene took over.

"I'm kinda pregnant," she said. "At least *I* know I am. Tom Junior doesn't believe I am. We want you to find out for sure."

"How do you expect me to know?" I said.

"You help Dr. Clinton a lot," she said, "so we thought maybe you had found out how to tell if a girl is pregnant."

"Why don't you go to a real doctor?" I said.

"We don't want anybody to know about it, that's why," Tom Junior said.

"But you just told me," I said.

"You don't count," he said, "You're just a kid

yourself."

"I'll do the best I can," I said. "When was your last period?"

"It's been a little over two months now," Bobby Lorene said.

"But she missed two months once before," Tom Junior said, "and it didn't mean a thing."

"That was when I had the flu," Bobby Lorene said, "This is different."

"Had you been exposed that time?" I said.

"No," she said, "up to that time we hadn't done anything but hold hands."

"Conception rarely takes place through the fingertips," I said.

"You sounded just like a doctor when you said that," she said. "I'll bet you've picked up a lot about doctoring— working here at the drug-store and helping all the doctors."

"I reckon I've learned a little," I said.

"Could you deliver a baby if I had one?" she said.

"Good Lord no," I said, "I'm not *that* far along."

"For Christ's sake, don't talk that way, Bobby Lorene," Tom Junior said. "You're not going to *have* a baby."

"That's what you think," she said, "I'll bet a million dollars I'm going to have a baby."

"Aren't those rubbers I bought from you guaranteed?" Tom Junior said.

"Guaranteed to do what?" I said.

"I mean guaranteed not to break," he said.

"We don't guarantee them," I said, "Maybe the manufacturer does."

"What good is that going to do me?" he said.

"I'll give you his name and address and you can write to him about the matter," I said.

"That won't change the fact that I'm pregnant,"

Bobby Lorene said.

"Don't *say* that!" Tom Junior said, "You *can't* be pregnant."

"I'll bet a million dollars I am," she said.

Tom Junior looked very unhappy and I felt sorry for him.

"I'll be honest with you-all," I said, "I don't really know how to tell whether Bobby Lorene is pregnant or not, so I can't help you much. But maybe Bill Kinney can. He's been working here at the drug-store for two years, off and on, and he knows a lot more about things like that than I do. I could telephone him and get him down here in a few minutes if you'd like for me to do that."

"I don't like for any more people to know about this," Tom Junior said.

"You'd better get him," Bobby Lorene said. "We've got to find out about this before it goes any further."

"I guess so," Tom Junior said.

I called Bill on the telephone and told him I had an interesting case and would like to have him in for consultation. He lived just two blocks from the drug-store, so he got there in a very few minutes.

"What's the nature of the case?" he said.

"Suspected pregnancy," I said, "Bobby Lorene has reason to believe that she is at least slightly pregnant."

"That's right," Bobby Lorene said.

"How is this gentleman involved?" Bill said, pointing at Tom Junior.

"He is the suspected expectant father," I said.

"I'm not anything of the kind," Tom Junior said.

"I get the idea," Bill said, "a sort of unwilling expectant father."

"Unenthusiastic, to say the least," I said.

"What are the symptoms?" Bill said.

"The patient has not had a period for over two

months now," I said, "and the suspected expectant father, I may add, has in effect admitted to a great rubber failure."

"I didn't admit anything of the kind," Tom Junior said, "I simply said weren't these rubbers you sell here guaranteed."

"Any morning sickness yet?" Bill said to Bobby Lorene.

"I'll tell the world there has been," Bobby Lorene said. "I've been nauseated every morning for a week."

"Take fruit juice for that," Bill said.

"Take lots of it," I said.

"Now look here," Tom Junior said, "You all are getting her more pregnant every minute!"

"I feel confident that the patient is pregnant," Bill said, "but I can't be absolutely sure without a local examination, of course."

"What's a 'local examination?'" Bobby Lorene said.

"That's an examination of the vagina, the uterus, and related organs," Bill said. He was good at reeling off those big medical words. It sounded just like he knew what he was talking about.

"Does that mean I have to take off my panties?" Bobby Lorene said.

"That's correct," Bill said.

"Can I do it here?" she said.

"We'll go back to the examining room," Bill said. He led the way back to Mr. Gates' dark room — the room where he tested people's eyes for glasses. All of us went along. Bill turned on the lights.

"You lie here on this table," he told Bobby Lorene. She climbed up on the table and stretched out on her back.

"I don't like this," Tom Junior said. "Couldn't she just *tell* you about those things and not have you looking at them?"

"No reputable physician would offer a diagnosis without a thorough examination," Bill said.

"Are you ready for me to take off my panties?" Bobby Lorene said.

"You may proceed." Bill said.

He got a new pair of rubber gloves out of stock and started putting one on his right hand. Bobby Lorene peeled off her panties. She did stick out behind. I mean she had a really gorgeous rump.

"I don't like this," Tom Junior said. "Couldn't you look the other way while you're examining her?"

"Of course, he couldn't," Bobby Lorene said. "Don't be any dumber than usual, Tom Junior." She talked to him just like he was already her husband.

Bill rubbed Vaseline on the thumb and first finger of the rubber glove on his right hand.

"Are you going to stick that — " Tom Junior said.

"I am," Bill said.

"I don't like that," Tom Junior said. "I don't trust the rubber goods you have in this store."

"Remember I'm already pregnant," Bobby Lorene said. Bill went ahead with the examination.

"That feels funny," Bobby Lorene said.

"Shut up," Tom Junior said.

"I guess I know how it feels," Bobby Lorene said.

Bill finished and started taking off the glove.

"The patient is definitely pregnant," he said. "The mouth of the uterus is noticeably enlarged and there are all of the other indications of early pregnancy."

"I told you so," Bobby Lorene said.

"I didn't feel anything enlarged in there," Tom Junior said. "It was all as tight as could be."

"That was because I was a virgin then just like I told you," Bobby Lorene said.

"Couldn't she *take* something?" Tom Junior said.

"That would be abortion," Bill said. "No reputable

physician would permit it. Not after the first month anyway. You two better get married as quick as you can."

"Married!" Tom Junior howled. "If I was to marry her, my folks — especially my mother — would take my hide off and hang it on the fence and pour salt on me."

"That's not a medical problem," Bill said. "I don't feel competent to advise you on it."

"We could go up to Mr. Klim's house tonight and get him to come down to his office and sell us the license — it's just a dollar and a half—and any of the preachers will be glad to marry us for two dollars," Bobby Lorene said. "You've got three dollars and a half, haven't you, Tom Junior?"

"Speaking of money, I want it expressly understood," Bill said, "that there are no charges for my service. They are a free-will offering gratis, since I am not licensed to practice medicine.

Bobby Lorene put her panties back on and got up off the table. "You have got three dollars and a half, haven't you, Tom Junior?" she said. "For if you haven't, I have."

I got the idea that Bobby Lorene didn't especially mind being pregnant and having to marry Tom Junior. After all, Tom Junior's father was next to the wealthiest man in town, and it was just a matter of time till Tom Junior was going to get that Hudson Super-Six. They went out the front door still talking about the three dollars and a half.

I understand that Bobby Lorene had to use her own money; but anyway they did get married that night, and it turned out that she was pregnant, just like Bill said she was. Tom Junior's parents threatened to disinherit him for marrying Bobby Lorene, and her father threatened to shoot him for not marrying her sooner, so Tom Junior had a hard life there for a while.

But to get back to the Thursday night in question. Just after Tom Junior and Bobby Lorene left the drugstore, Mr. John Barker came in. I think he had been waiting out in front. He was walking spraddle-legged and limping like he was mighty bad off.

"Cary," he said, "I'm in a hell of a shape. I'm so sore and swelled up that I can't ride a horse, much less walk."

"Mr. Barker," I said. "I told you that stuff wouldn't do you a speck of good."

"I reckon you're right," he said, "but what am I going to do now? If my wife finds out about this, she'll shoot me first and divorce me later."

"You need to go to a hospital, Mr. Barker," I said. "Why don't you make a business trip down to Fort Worth and go to the Methodist Hospital as soon as you get there?"

"Cary," he said, "that's the best idea you ever had. I'll catch the midnight train tonight and be there early in the morning. I'll phone my wife and tell her I've just heard of a chance to buy a trainload of stocker steers at a good price. Cary, you're the brightest boy I've ever known. Here, take this ten dollar bill."

"No sir, Mr. Barker," I said, "I can't take pay for giving medical advice. You see, I'm not licensed to practice medicine."

"Well, give me one of them ten dollar packages of chewing gum then," he said. He slammed a ten dollar bill down on the counter and picked up a package of Spearmint and headed out the front door.

At the door he stopped and turned around. "Cary," he said, "Ain't there some other good hospital in Fort Worth besides the Methodist Hospital? My wife's a Methodist, and I'd rather the Methodists didn't know anything about this on that account."

"Try St. Joseph's," I said, "it's Catholic."

"That's fine," he said, "I don't know no Catholics. Catholics ain't like Methodists anyway."

He headed down toward the depot.

I put a nickel in the cash register for the chewing gum and put the ten dollar bill in my pocket. The next Sunday night I wadded it up tight and put it in the collection plate at the Christian Church. Mr. Launcelot Jones, who always takes up the collection at our church, saw it when he started to count the money and fainted and had to be carried out of the church and taken home and put to bed and given stimulants. He wasn't able to go back to work till Wednesday, so maybe it would have been better if I had just kept that ten dollar bill in spite of the ethics of the American Medical Association. It's so hard to know what's right sometimes.

The next Thursday night Dem Witt came in again. He sidled back to the prescription counter where I was just like he had the first time, and he looked all around again before he said anything and then he used that same stage whisper.

"Cary," he said, "I've been wearing this thing for two weeks, and I don't have a sign of disease of any kind. Don't you think it would be safe for me to take it off now?"

## A Lesson in Obstetrics

During that winter there was a big influenza epidemic in Kiowa County and all over the country. All the doctors had been run ragged for days and weeks. One night the telephone rang at the drug-store and I answered it. It was Dr. Clinton.

"Cary, is Dr. Hartlock there?" he asked.

"No, he isn't," I said, "I haven't seen him since early this morning. You know how it's been lately."

"Yes, I know," he said, "I don't suppose you know where he went?"

"No sir, I don't, Doctor. I don't have the least idea," I said.

"Well, in that case you'll have to do something for me, Cary," he said. "I'm out here at Bob Williford's house, about fifteen miles south of town on the Hog Mountain road. His wife is in labor but things aren't going right. I may have to try a Caesarian, and I wanted Dr. Hartlock to help me."

He stopped talking and I said, "Yes sir."

"Cary," he said, " You go up to my office and get my surgical kit and anything else you see around that you think I might need. And bring me two cans of ether from the drug-store. You can borrow Mr. Brown's car to drive out here. If you have any trouble finding the place, you can ask along the way."

"Yes sir, Doctor," I said, "I'll be out there as soon as I can."

I told Mr. Brown what Dr. Clinton wanted  me to do and he said to do it. I went up to Dr. Clinton's office and gathered up all the stuff I could find. I brought it down and put it in Mr. Brown's car.

And then I drove    out south    of town. For the first few miles the road was graveled, but    that stopped at the Horse Creek bridge, and after that it was mostly mud. That Ford slipped and slithered all over the road. I drove in low as much as I did in high. The radiator boiled even in the cold weather, and I could smell the denatured alcohol evaporating.

Down in a low place just after I turned off onto the Hog Mountain road, I got stuck completely. Both back wheels spun and one of the front wheels was behind a big rock. I got out and jacked up one back wheel after the other and put mud chains on them. Then I dug the big rock out from in front of the front wheel and rolled it over to the side of the road. The mud chains took hold after they'd dug down to solid ground.

I didn't know where Bob Williford lived so I stopped at the next house to ask. I stopped out in front and started walking up toward the house. Three big dogs and four pups ran out and started barking at me. One of the big dogs acted like he meant business so I patted him and talked to him and finally got him to change his mind about chewing me up. Then I called "Hello" at the house.

After a minute or two a man came to the font door.

"Somebody out there?" he said.

"Yessir," I said, "I'm looking for Bob Williford's place. Could you tell me where he lives?"

"Yes," he said, "Bob lives about three or four miles on up the road. You go on up here about a mile and a half or maybe two miles and you turn to the left. There's a lane there that goes up through the old Callaway Ranch. After you get back in there about a mile, you come to a gate. You go through that gate and there are two trails. One goes off to the right and the other one off to the left. The one that goes to the left is purty dim because Bob is the only one that uses it. But that's the one you want to take. You may miss it in the dark, but anyway that's the one you want to take."

"I'm much obliged to you." I said. "Now let me see if

I've got it straight." I said it all back to him as nearly as I could.

"That's right," he said. "Is something the matter over at Bob's house?"

"His wife is having a baby," I said. "Dr. Clinton is over there but things aren't going right, so he phoned for me to bring him some things he needs."

"That's too bad," the man said. "Maybe I better go with you to be sure you get there right quick."

"I think I can find it," I said.

"You just wait till I get my pants on," he said, "and I'll ride over there with you. Bob might need some help anyway."

"I don't want to put you to any trouble," I said.

"No trouble at all," he said, "just wait till I get my pants on."

He went back into the house and lighted a lamp. In just a minute or two he was back out with his clothes on.

"My name is Asa Greer," he said.

"I'm Cary McKelvey," I said. "I work in Mr. Brown's drug-store in Kiowa."

"Yes, I think I've seen you there," he said. "I know Mr. Brown well — traded with him for years."

He climbed into the Ford and we drove off. The road got better, mostly because it was on high ground and the water had drained off.

"This is Bob's and Bessie's first baby," Mr. Greer said. "They've just been married about a year."

"There's apt to be trouble with the first one," I said.

"Yes I reckon there is," he said, "but you wouldn't think Bessie would be the kind to have trouble that a way. She's a big girl — broad shouldered and broad hipped. Mostly it's the little skinny ones that have trouble having a young-un."

"That's right," I said.

We got to the house without any trouble, but I surely was glad Mr. Greer was with me, because it would have been mighty easy to get lost in the dark. There were people all over the place already — mostly women but several men too. The women were in the house and the men were out in the front yard standing around a fire.

I got Dr. Clinton's things out of the car and carried them in. Dr. Clinton was in the bedroom with Bessie Williford. There were several women in there too.

"Come in, Cary," Dr. Clinton said.

"How are things going, Doctor?" I said.

"No better than when I called you," he said, "in fact, worse. Do you have a stethoscope there?"

"I think so," I said and fished it out of the pile.

"I want to take a listen at her heart," he said, "and then I'll take her blood pressure."

He listened a while and then he wrapped the blood pressure thing around her arm and pumped it up. Her blood pressure was 250.

"That's mighty high, isn't it, Doctor?" I said.

"That's desperately high," he said. "She's been in hard labor for over nine hours now, and she hasn't done a bit of good. Her pelvic bones are too close together, front to back."

"I know what I'd do if I was in charge here," an old woman down at the other end of the room said. Dr. Clinton didn't pay any attention to her. I looked at the old woman. She looked like a witch if I ever saw anybody who did.

"Who's that, Doctor?" I said.

"That's old Granny Gilman," he said. "She's an old fashioned midwife. I run into her ever so often around here. People don't use her much anymore, but she still likes to come around whenever a baby's being born. I don't pay any attention to her—just let her talk."

"She looks like Mrs. Devil herself," I said.

"She's a good-hearted old soul," the doctor said. "I don't pay any attention to her."

Bessie Williford started moaning again.

"Cary, do you think you could give an anesthetic?" Doctor Clinton said.

"I don't know, Doctor," I said, "I've seen you do it several times."

"I think you're going to have to give one," he said. "This girl isn't going to make it by herself."

"I'll try it," I said.

"I'm going in here and drink a cup of coffee and eat a little something." the Doctor said. "I haven't had a bite to eat since breakfast this morning. And when I've done that, we'll try a Caesarian. The conditions here aren't ideal, by any means, but we'll have to try it."

"You go ahead, Doctor," I said. "You must be plenty empty."

"I am empty," he said, "and sort of tired, too. I called on a lot of flu patients before I came out here."

"The coffee is ready, Doctor," Bessie Williford's mother said, "and I've sliced you some ham and there's some butterbeans and some collards and a few sweet potatoes and a custard pie I baked yesterday. I'm sorry I didn't get over here in time to cook up some fittin' food for you."

"That'll be more than enough, Mrs. Smith," the doctor said. "I can't take but a few minutes anyway."

He went out to the kitchen with her, and I walked over to the fireplace to warm my hands. They were still cold from the drive.

"I ought to wash my hands if I am going to give that anesthetic," I said to myself. My hands still had mud on them from putting the chains on the back wheels.

"Could I wash my hands?" I asked one of the women. "Dr. Clinton wants me to help him when he comes back."

"There's some warm water right in here," the woman said. "I'll pour you a pan-full."

I went with her and washed my hands and dried them. I couldn't have been gone more than two or three minutes. When I got back I noticed that old Granny Gilman was over by the bed where Bessie Williford was lying. She had something in her hand that looked about like a pencil. She took a bottle of snuff out of her apron pocket and dipped the thing in the snuff. Then she stooped down and stuck one end of it up Bessie Williford's nose. Before I could do anything to stop her, she blew on the other end.

And then the queerest thing happened. Bessie Williford began to sneeze. You never heard such sneezing in your life. She doubled up and jerked and twisted and sneezed. And then she did it all over again.

"It's a comin'," Granny Gilman cackled, "It's a comin'!"

"What in the world did you do to her?" I said.

"I snuffed her," she said; "It'll work when nothin' else in the world will. It's a comin'."

"What do you mean you 'snuffed her'?" I said.

"I blew snuff up her nose with a turkey quill," she said, "to make her sneeze. It's a comin'."

I looked at the bed. And that was the first time I ever saw a baby born. By the time Dr. Clinton got back into the room, Granny Gilman was holding a baby boy up by his hind legs and spanking him to make him cry. He cried in a big way.

"I don't like to do a woman that a way," Granny said, "but I could see that you all didn't know what to do next. That rip in Bessie's crotch will grow up."

"I can do something about that," Dr. Clinton said, and he began to get out a needle and some sutures. "You won't have to give that anesthetic after all, Cary."

“That suits me,” I said.

For just then I realized that I had forgotten to bring the two cans of ether the doctor wanted, but I didn’t see any use telling him that under the circumstances.

# Dr. Hellums and Miss Penelope

Dr. Hellums came back. He had been gone from Kiowa for a year or so on one of his medicine selling trips. But as he always did, he came back. He drove his horse and buggy up in front of the drug-store and called me to come out and help him. His legs were paralyzed, so he had to get somebody to help him out of his buggy.

I had known him a long time before I started working at the drug-store, but I never had had a chance to talk to him much. He sat down in Mr. Brown's rocking chair by the cigar case and took off his derby.

"How did you get your medical education, Doctor?" I said.

"It's a long story, son," he said. "I've been paralyzed since I was a small boy. I couldn't do ordinary work, so I had to look around for a career that fitted my circumstances. I tried making counterfeit money at first, but I had hard luck. They caught me and sent me to the federal penitentiary for that. But since I couldn't do manual labor of any kind, the warden put me to work as a clerk in the hospital. I got interested in medicine and started reading books about it and practicing on the convicts in the hospital. When my five years were up, I took the State Board examination and passed it. So I've been practicing medicine for thirty years now."

"Do you do surgery, too?" I said.

"Minor surgery," he said. "I remove corns and ingrowing toenails, but I'm not much on major surgery. Mostly I have specialized in internal medicine, you might say."

"I see," I said.

"In fact," he said, "I've got a new formula out there

now that I want you to bottle up for me. Go out and look in the back of the buggy and bring in the jug."

"Yes sir," I said. I went out to the buggy and found a big five-gallon glass jug back of the seat. It was full of something that looked like iced tea. I brought it in.

"What do you want done with this, Doctor?" I said.

"Make me up about six dozen eight-ounce bottles of it," he said. "I want to try it out around here before I go on my next trip. Here are the labels for it."

He handed me a package of printed labels. I read one of them. It said:

"Dr. Hellums' Spring Tonic, System Purifier, and Indigestion Specific Effective in the Relief of Malaria, Asthma, Back-Ache, Dizziness, Shortness of Breath, Acid Stomach, Cholera Morbus, Diarrhea, Constipation, All Forms of Indigestion, Head-Ache, Rheumatism, Piles, Heart Trouble, Loss of Manhood, Female Complaints, and Dandruff—Take two tablespoonfuls in half a glass of water before each meal."

"Isn't it good for cancer, too?" I said.

"I have a special salve for cancer," Dr. Hellums said.

"What did you sell last trip?" I said.

"This last time I was selling Dr. Hellums' Body Renovator, Bile Regulator, and First Aid to Animals," he said.

"What was it like?" I said.

"It was about the same as this one except that it was also good for heaves, spavins, sway-backedness, and other ailments of the horse," he said.

"Why did you change it?" I said.

"With automobiles all over the place like they are now, there are so few horses left it don't hardly pay to include them," he said.

"I think I can get this bottled up for you this afternoon," I said.

"That'll be fine," he said, "I'll be around for it some

time tomorrow."

I helped him back into his buggy and he drove off.

I carried the big jug back to the prescription case and opened it. If I was any judge of such matters, it had plenty of *spirits frumenti* in it. It smelled like Jake Morgan's still in hot weather. I got out a carton of eight-ounce bottles and began filling them up with it. I worked at it between customers most of the afternoon.

Late that afternoon Miss Penelope Brandon came in. She was Colonel Brandon's old-maid daughter. I don't know why she hadn't ever gotten married, but I don't think it was because she didn't want to. She was about forty years old and beginning to be a little plump. She had enjoyed poor health for years, and all the doctors in town had had a try at her, but they hadn't done her a speck of good. She still had all the symptoms she'd started out with and maybe some more.

"Cary," she said, "my neurasthenia is worse than usual today. I could go to a doctor, of course, but I'm waiting for that new chiropractor to get his office opened up before I do any more doctoring. I've already given every doctor in this town all the chance he deserves to cure me, and not one of them has helped me, so I'm not going to any of them anymore. But I *do* need something to get me through the rest of this day. Don't you have something that will relieve my neurasthenia?"

"Miss Penelope," I said, "we've got just what you need. We got in a whole shipment of a new neurasthenia specific just this morning. I'll get a bottle of it for you."

I went back to the prescription case and got a bottle of Dr. Hellums cure-all and typed a special label for it. I called it "Ajax Neurasthenia Specific." I brought it out to Miss Penelope.

"Miss Penelope," I said, "the usual dose of this is two

tablespoonfuls before each meal; but since you're so far behind on the treatment of your case, if I were you I'd start out right now taking a half a glass of it and keep it up at that rate till you've finished the first bottle. Then you can take the second one at the regular dosage."

"I believe I'll do that," she said. "Could you fix me the first dose now?"

"Sure," I said. I went up to the soda fountain and poured a Coca-Cola glass half full of the Specific. Miss Penelope drank it and didn't choke but twice.

"It seems a little strong," she said, "but I believe I feel better already."

"You just keep on taking it that way," I said, "and I'm sure you'll feel a lot better."

"I'll do it religiously," she said and tucked the bottle under her arm. She went out the front door with a lilt in her step.

Just after I got back to the drug-store after supper that night, Miss Penelope came in again. She had color in her face and a light in her eyes that didn't look a bit like Miss Penelope Brandon.

"Cary," she said, "I've finished the birst fottle and it's done me so much good I want another one right now."

"Sure, Miss Penelope," I said, "I'll get you one." I went back and labeled another bottle and brought it out to her.

"I can see that it's helped you a lot, Miss Penelope," I said, "but I believe you'd better wait till in the morning to take another dose. It's pretty powerful medicine, you know."

"I'll take just one more dose now," she said, "and then I'll wait till tomorrow. But I feel that I need to continue the treatment just now. If you'll just give me a glass—"

I brought her a Coca-Cola glass and she sat down at one of the ice-cream tables and opened the new bottle.

She poured out a generous half a glass and began to sip it.

Mr. Thad Grainger came in to buy a cigar and I had to wait on him. It took him a long time to make up his mind about what kind of cigar he wanted. He pinched most of them in four boxes before he finally picked one out. And then I had to talk politics with him while he cut the ends off and lighted it.

"I hear that old Dr. Wilbarger's going to run for the legislature again this year," he said.

"Yes sir, he says he's going to," I said.

"If he'd get a haircut and pull up his pants, he might get elected," he said.

"That ought to help," I said.

"Tell him I don't think I'm going to vote for him if the price of cotton don't go up between now and election time," he said.

"Yes sir," I said, "I'll tell him."

When I got back to Miss Penelope, she'd poured herself another glass and was making real progress on it.

"I don't believe I'd take anymore of that now, Miss Penelope," I said. "I don't want you to overdo this treatment."

She looked at me sort of funny and giggled.

"Cary," she said, "you're one of the best looking young men I've ever known. I've admired you ever since I've known you."

"You have me mixed up with somebody else," I said.

"Of course, I'm a few years older than you," she said, "but that shouldn't keep us from having a beautiful friendship. Now should it?"

"Of course not, Miss Penelope," I said, "I've always liked you fine. But I believe you'd better — "

Old Mr. Jeeter came in to get a package of mentholated cough drops. He ate them like candy. I had to wait on him and listen to his latest prediction about when the world was going to come to an end. He re-read the Book of Revelation every few days and usually came up with a new notion about the end of the world. He liked to tell people about his ideas and the arguments in favor of them. And since he was one of our steadiest customers, I felt like I ought to listen to him.

When I got back to Miss Penelope this time, she was going on her third glass, and the situation looked bad. She had propped one foot up on a chair in front of her and her supporter was showing above her stocking-top. I figured that if I didn't get her out of there before Mr. Brown got back from supper I was surely going to have a lot of explaining to do.

"Miss Penelope," I said, "I believe you'd better go home. Sometimes the night air has a mighty bad effect on neurasthenia patients when they've just started this new treatment."

"Cary," She said sort of dreamy like, "I may not go home tonight. I feel that I would like to roam the streets in search of adventure —and romance. Or could you take me home?"

"I'd love to take you home, Miss Penelope," I said, "but I can't leave the drug-store. Mr. Brown isn't here."

"That's the first time you've said you love me," she said.

"I said I'd love to take you home," I said.

"It's all the same," she said.

"Not quite," I said.

"I feel a new freedom," she said — "a freedom I have never felt before. I'm as free as the birds that air in the fly."

She climbed up in the chair she'd been sitting in and heisted her skirt up to her knees.

"I should like to do the Highland Fling," she said, "as

I did when I was a child."

"You'd better get down from there before somebody comes in, Miss Penelope," I said.

"I shall never get down," she said, "I shall climb higher and higher up to the stars."

She climbed up on the ice-cream table and heisted her skirt a little higher.

And then the worst happened. The front door opened, and of all the people in world to come in, who was it but Colonel Brandon himself! He walked back toward the back of the drug-store and saw Miss Penelope standing up on that ice-cream table with her skirt up around her waist.

"Penny," he said, "what in the pluperfect hell are you doing up there?"

"I am doing the Highland Fling, pappy," she said. And she kicked the Colonel's hat off.

"Get down from there before I blister your bottom," the Colonel said.

"I'll get down when I please," Miss Penelope said.

The Colonel grabbed at her and she dodged. When she dodged she lost her balance and fell into the candy case. It broke into ten million pieces. Miss Penelope went out like a light.

"Help me carry her out to the car, son," the Colonel said, "and for Christ's sake, don't ever tell anybody about this. I'll square it with Mr. Brown about the candy case."

I helped him carry Miss Penelope out to the car. At the front door she whispered, "Hold me closely, Cary dear."

"What's that?" Colonel Brandon said.

"Nothing," I said.

We wadded Miss Penelope into the back seat of the car.

"About that stuff Penny was drinking" the Colonel

said, "it must have been pretty good to get her up on that table. Have you got anymore of it, son?"

"Plenty, Colonel," I said.

"Fix me up about two dozen bottles of it," he said. "With this damn Prohibition we've got now, a gentleman has to stoop pretty low."

# The Zipper

Mr. Harold Blankenship and Miss Bernice Willbank came into the drug-store and sat down at one of the ice cream tables. Mr. Blankenship was the new assistant pastor at the Baptist Church and Miss Bernice had played the organ at the church for a long time. She was about the same age as Miss Penelope Brandon. In fact, she and Miss Penelope were close friends and had a great deal in common. But Miss Bernice had been making real progress since Mr. Blankenship came to town. He was a bachelor and he had taken an interest in Miss Bernice ever since their first choir practice together. This particular afternoon she had been helping him decorate the church for the Easter service the next Sunday.

They ordered two lime-aides; and while she was drinking hers, he excused himself and went back to the Men's Room in the back of the drug-store.

I was busy waiting on some other customers at the time and didn't pay any attention to him. But after five minutes I noticed that he was still gone. Miss Bernice finished her lime-aide and twisted up the straw and he still hadn't come back. Some more customers came in and some of them spoke to Miss Bernice and wondered why she was sitting there by herself. I could see that Miss Bernice was wondering too.

I thought maybe I'd better take a look in the back room.

I looked back there but Mr. Blankenship wasn't in sight. The door to the Men's Room was closed. I walked up close to it and said, "Are you all right, Mr. Blankenship?"

There wasn't any answer. I tried the door and it was locked on the inside. I called to Mr. Blankenship again but he still didn't answer. I went up to the front and got Mr. Brown.

"Maybe you'd better come back here a minute, Mr. Brown," I said. "Mr. Blankenship is in the toilet and he didn't answer when I called him."

"Are you sure he's in there?" Mr. Brown said.

"He's in there if he didn't go out the back door," I said, "and besides the door is locked from the inside. Somebody is in there."

"Are you all right, Reverend?" Mr. Brown said.

But the Reverend didn't answer. Mr. Brown knocked on the door. There was still no answer.

"This bothers me," Mr. Brown said. He knocked harder. But it didn't do any good.

"Are you sure he's in there, Cary?" Mr. Brown said.

"I don't know where else he could be," I said.

Just then we heard a faint moan from inside the toilet.

"He's fainted," Mr. Brown said, "We'll have to break the door down!"

I got a two-by-four that we used to bar the back door and used it as a battering ram. The second time I hit it, the door splintered away from the lock. It made an awful noise and most of the men who regularly loafed in front of the soda fountain came running back to see what had happened. Mr. Blankenship was sprawled across the toilet seat unconscious.

At first we couldn't figure what had happened to him; but when we carried him out and put him on a table, we saw what it was. The zipper on the fly of his trousers had been pulled up so as to catch a strip of the loose skin on the underside of his penis. Don't ask me how he happened to do it. I guess he had his mind on something else when he started to close the zipper. Anyway he had done it and then fainted from the pain.

"Run get Dr. Clinton as quick as you can," Mr. Brown

said.

I ran through the front of the drug-store.

"What happened, Cary?" Miss Bernice said.

"A bad accident, Miss Bernice," I said, "You mustn't go back there."

I ran up to Dr. Clinton's office and told him what had happened. He began gathering up his things. He looked worried.

"I've never had a case like this before," he said. "I don't know much about these zippers. I have one on my tobacco pouch but I didn't know they'd started putting them on trousers."

"Yes, Doctor, they've been doing that for the last year or two now'." I said. "The pants to my new suit have a zipper on them."

"As if a doctor's life wasn't hard enough without their inventing those things," he said.

He took his regular pill bag and a handful of surgical instruments. He didn't know what he was going to need. We went back through the front of the drug-store, and I could see that Miss Bernice was getting panicky.

"Doctor, what has happened to Mr. Blankenship?" she said.

"Frankly, I don't know, Miss Bernice," the doctor said, "I wish I did."

That made Miss Bernice more panicky than she was before.

We went on back to where the patient was. He was still unconscious. Dr. Clinton looked him over.

"We'll give him a local anesthetic," he said, "and then we'll try to get this thing loose."

He took out a hypodermic needle, loaded it, and gave Mr. Blankenship a shot where it would do him the most good. He waited a little while for it to take effect, and then he began to fumble with the zipper.

About that time Mr. Blankenship came to. Evidently he couldn't feel anything where the doctor had given him the anesthetic, so he thought it was gone.

"Doctor," he said, "I'm sorry you had to amputate. Miss Bernice promised just this afternoon to be my wife; and I feel sure she will want children."

"Take it easy," Dr. Clinton said, "I haven't amputated anything yet, but I may have to. I can't make heads or tails of this contraption. It's jammed — it won't go backward or forward."

"Then there is still hope," Mr. Blankenship said.

"Yes, there is still hope, such as it is," Dr. Clinton said. He went on fumbling with the zipper. The whole combination was so limp and flimsy that it was hard to do anything with it. The doctor didn't know what to hold onto and what to pull. I felt sorry for him.

"Maybe, doctor," I said, "this isn't a medical job. Maybe we ought to get a mechanic. A mechanic ought to know how those zippers work."

"You're exactly right, Cary," Dr. Clinton said. "This isn't a job for a doctor; it's a job for a dress-maker!"

"Better make it a tailor instead of a dress-maker, considering the location," I said.

"You're right," he said. "Run over and get Happy Hemphill."

Happy Hemphill had a tailor shop over on the west side of the square, and I started over there to get him.

As I passed Miss Bernice, she said, "Cary, I simply cannot stand this suspense any longer — what *has* happened to Mr. Blankenship."

"Miss Bernice," I said, "you'll have to ask the doctor. I couldn't give you the correct term for it even if I wanted to." And I kept running.

There was a bunch of loafers in Happy's shop when I got there, just as there always was; and, of course, they heard me when I told Happy what had happened to Mr.

Blankenship and what the doctor wanted Happy to do. Happy picked up a big pair of shears, reached down under his press, brought out the bottle of white lightning he kept there, took a long swig of it, and said. "Cary, I'm ready to go."

We started over toward the drug-store, cutting across the square to save time, and all the loafers followed us. Happy was in front with the big shears.

About half way across the square, he began to sing "Onward, Christian Soldiers!" as loud as he could sing. The procession attracted a good deal of attention, and other people joined it to see what was happening.

When we went into the drug-store again, Miss Bernice was positively terrified.

"Cary, I simply must know," she said, "no matter how bad it is."

"It won't be long now, Miss Benice," Happy said, snapping the big scissors, "as the monkey said when he backed into the lawn mower."

The back room was already full of people so that we could hardly get through them; and then all of Happy's bunch crowded in, too.

"Dr. Clinton, please get these people out of here," Mr. Blankenship said. "I feel that I am suffocating."

"Mr. Brown, get these people out of here," Dr. Clinton said. "The patient might suffocate."

"Cary, get these people out of here," Mr. Brown said. "Gentlemen, will you please leave," I said, "The patient's life is in danger."

But nobody left. Those nearest the table pushed back a little, and those at the back pushed forward a little to try to see what was going on. But nobody left.

"Cary, go get the city marshal," Mr. Brown said. "We've got to get these people out of here."

I wiggled my way through the crowd and started out through the front of the drug-store again. Miss Bernice was now pretty close to hysterics. She started to say something to me but I didn't even stop this time. I ran up to the city hall to find Hawkshaw Cummins, the city marshal. In Kiowa the city hall and the fire station are in the same building. Hawkshaw and Bob Holland, the fire chief, were playing checkers. There were about a dozen other men sitting around the place. I told Hawkshaw that Dr. Clinton was performing an emergency operation in the backroom of the drug-store and that we needed him to make the crowd leave and to keep them from coming back.

"And you need to come quick, Mr. Cummins," I said, "This is serious."

"I'll drive you down in the fire truck," Bob Holland said, "You can ride with us, Cary."

We all jumped into the front seat of the fire truck; but before Bob could get it out of the station, most of the other men had swung on behind. As we rounded the corner of the square, Bob pulled the siren wide open, so when we got to the drug-store, the rest of the town was there to meet us.

I led the way into the drug-store, and the city marshal and the fire chief followed me. Miss Bernice looked at them and started screaming. That helped to attract more people into the drug-store. Some people somehow got the idea that she had been criminally assaulted in the back room. They didn't really think that it was the new preacher who had done it, but they hoped it was.

Back in the back room Hawkshaw started trying to get the people out. But every time he got one out the front, two more came in at the back. By this time people thought there was a fire and a fight in the back of the drug-store, so we had the biggest crowd since the time Joe Bailey made a speech in his campaign for governor.

I got over to the table where the patient was, but I could see that Happy wasn't doing much good. He had cut the zipper loose from the trousers, but he still didn't have it loose from Mr. Blankenship.

"That's the part I don't know about, Doctor," he said, "I never have worked on that part before."

"That makes two of us who haven't," Dr. Clinton said, "We've got to get more talent on this job."

"How about a tinsmith?" I said. "Do you reckon Claude Benson could help? He's a good sheet-metal worker."

"Maybe he could," Dr. Clinton said. "At least, he couldn't do any worse than Happy and I have. Run over and get him, Cary."

I ran out through the front of the drug-store again. Miss Bernice was still screaming and people were still fighting their way into the drug-store to see what was the matter with her. It was all I could do to get out the front door.

I ran clear across the square and down two blocks to Claude Benson's tin shop. It took me a long time to explain to Claude what had happened and what we wanted him to do. He had never seen or heard of one of these newfangled zippers, and he wasn't sure he wanted to get mixed up with any such stuff. He said he liked making milk coolers best, and he had plenty of decent work like that to do without getting involved with zippers and Baptist preachers.

"But the poor man is suffering terribly," I said, "Just think how you'd feel if you were in his place."

"All right," Claude said, "I'll go and see what I can do. But I can tell you to start with that I don't know a thing in the world about it. I don't lay no claim to bein' an educated man."

He gathered up a whole toolkit full of tools and a blowtorch. The blowtorch was lighted and he didn't turn it out. We got into his pick-up truck and drove over to the drugstore and parked by the fire truck. That lighted blowtorch did serve one purpose. It scattered the crowd when we started into the drugstore with it. But it had a bad effect on Miss Bernice. When she saw Claude Benson with that lighted blowtorch, it was the last straw for her. She fainted and turned over backward into the new candy case. It broke into about the same number of pieces the old one had when Miss Penelope fell on top of it. We did have the worst luck with candy cases that year.

When the candy case broke it made so much noise that the crowd couldn't decide whether there was more excitement in the back room or the front room, so they began to divide their time between the two. Mr. Brown's drugstore really was a mess.

But Claude and the blowtorch finally cleared a path to the table where Mr. Blankenship was. I have always admired the way Claude took hold of the situation when he got there.

"You hold his water-works, doctor," he said, "and let me take a look at how this thing works."

He began to examine the teeth of the zipper to see how they fitted together. Then he reached down and got a pair of small wire cutters from his toolkit. In five minutes' time he had snipped each of the little prongs off the zipper and it was loose from Mr. Blankenship. The crowd got so interested in watching Claude they got right quiet, and when he had finished, they cheered like Kiowa had just made a touchdown in the Thanksgiving Day football game with Postoak City. Several men picked Claude up on their shoulders and carried him out through the front of the drugstore to his truck, and the rest of the crowd followed them.

Somebody then accidentally kicked the blowtorch over and it set fire to a packing case full of excelsior, so we did have a fire after all, but I threw a bucket of water on it and put it out before it could spread to the rest of the drugstore. It sure did make a mess on the floor, though.

When I went back up to the front, poor Miss Bernice was still lying in the shattered remains of the candy case. Nobody was paying any attention to her, so I dragged her out and laid her on the floor and pulled her dress down and went back to see if I could get Dr. Clinton to come and see about her. But he was busy sewing up Mr. Blankenship. I came back and treated Miss Bernice with Aromatic Spirits of Ammonia and finally got her revived.

"Take me to Mr. Blankenship at once," she said when she opened her eyes.

"The doctor is still operating on him, Miss Bernice," I said. "You can't see him for some time yet. You'd better go on home as soon as you feel well enough."

"I shall never leave him," she said. "I shall stay by his side and nurse him back to health. I am his betrothed."

"But if you want a happy married life with him," I said, "you'd better give him a little while to recover. You can start nursing him later on. He isn't in any condition to be nursed right now."

"I shall wait for him," she said.

I tried to argue with her but it didn't do any good. She wouldn't leave. Dr. Clinton got through sewing Mr. Blankenship up, but the Reverend still couldn't make a public appearance on account Happy had cut most of the front out of his trousers in getting the zipper out. So the doctor smuggled him out the back door and drove him home in his car. That left Miss Bernice completely stood up, so to speak, and I finally persuaded her to go on home.

I started cleaning up the broken glass from the candy case and the half-burned excelsior and the water in the backroom. I thought that Mr. Blankenship's accident had been pretty hard on the drugstore. But it turned out that it was a lot harder on him and Miss Bernice. It wasn't any time till everybody in town knew what had happened to him and some people were mighty unkind about it.

One man would say, "Did you hear what happened to the new Baptist preacher?"

And the other man would say, "Yes, I heard it but I don't believe it. I don't believe that could happen to a Baptist preacher because I don't believe he has one to begin with." And then they would both laugh all over the place.

What made it worse was that the Reverend was supposed to get married to Miss Bernice right away. There were so many inquiries about whether he was ready for married life yet that it got to where he just couldn't stand it. He stayed at home all the time so people couldn't ask him. And somehow Miss Bernice found out what had happened to him; and although she was loyal to him to the bitter end, I'm sure it was a source of much embarrassment to her. She sort of hesitated to be seen in public with him.

The bitter end came when Mr. Blankenship resigned his position with the Baptist Church, broke his engagement with Miss Bernice, and went back to East Texas where he had come from. It blighted Miss Bernice's life and caused the Baptists to lose out in competition with the Methodists in getting new church members for the next several years, which just goes to show what a little thing like a zipper getting caught can lead to. It reminded me of the poem about the lost horseshoe nail that finally led to the loss of a kingdom.

# The Simplex Magic Hair Curler

That first year I worked at the drug-store, my hair began to get curly as everything. My mother said it was because I had started combing it. She said I never had combed my hair till the night I graduated from high school. I don't know' what made it do it, but anyway it got curlier and curlier all that year.

Girls would come into the drugstore and look at me and say, "Cary, what in the world are you doing to your hair to make it so curly?"

I would say, "That's a trade secret."

One Saturday when several girls had asked me about my hair, Bill said, "We ought to make some money out of this. A lot of these girls are crazy enough to pay good money to get curly hair. I'm going to cash in on it."

"How do you mean?" I said.

"The next time some girl asks you what makes your hair so curly, you tell her that you use some stuff that Bill Kinney makes, and that if she wants some of it to see me about it."

"What're you going to sell them?" I said.

"I'll think up something," he said, "Probably Dr. Hellums can help me."

"What do I get out of it?" I said.

"The usual ten percent commission," he said.

"I think I ought to get more than that," I said, "I think I ought to get twenty percent."

"I'll give you ten percent of the first \$10,000 and twenty percent of all over \$10,000," he said.

So I did what Bill said. The next time a girl asked me how I made my hair curly, I said, "Now, Helen, if you really want to know, I'll tell you. I put some stuff on it that Bill Kinney makes up. You know how curly his hair is. It's been that way for years because he started using the stuff a long time ago. He'll probably sell you some of it if you really want it. But don't tell him I told you. And don't tell anybody else."

"Oh, I won't," she said, "and I do thank you."

In a week's time practically every girl in town had heard of Bill's hair-curling concoction, and he had dozens of orders. He told them at first that it would take him a little time to make up a new batch because some of the secret ingredients had to come from Africa.

"What in the world are you going to sell them?" I said.

"I've about got it figured out," he said. "It's going to have a glycerine base; that'll make their hair kink up. And then I'll put some collodion in it to hold the kinks after they form. And I'd better put a little ether in it to make it dry out quickly. And I'd better put something in it to make it smell good. Girls always want everything to smell good. I'm going to call it Kinney's Simplex Magic Hair Curler."

"When are you going to have it ready?" I said.

"About Saturday, I think," he said.

"Remember my ten percent," I said.

"Okay," he said.

Sure enough, he started making deliveries the next Saturday. He put the stuff in bottles and borrowed Spec Larson's Ford and delivered a bottle to all of the girls that had ordered one. He got a dollar a bottle for it, which ran into big money in a hurry.

Just after I got back to the drugstore after supper that night, the telephone rang and I answered it.

"Is Bill Kinney there?" a girl asked.

"No," I said, "Bill didn't work here today. He had some business of his own to attend to, I think."

"Yes, I know," the girl said, "He sold me a bottle of that hair-curling stuff of his and do you know what it has done to my hair?"

"No, I don't," I said, "What has it done?"

"It turned my hair green," she said, "a bright, shiny green. And all that I want with him is to find out how to get rid of that green color, and then I'll sort of kill him."

"I'm sure there must be some mistake," I said. "I've used it for months and it never has turned my hair green. You must not have followed the directions."

"All the directions said was to put it on," she said, "and that's all I did. Where is Bill Kinney? That's what I want to know."

"I don't know," I said, "He might be at home."

"I'll try there," she said and hung up.

Well, that was just the beginning. During the next fifteen minutes that telephone rang fifteen times, and every time it was a girl wanting to know where she could find Bill to kill him and also how to get the green out of her hair. Just as it was ringing for the sixteenth time, Bill came running in through the back door.

"You've been wanted on the telephone," I said.

"Yes, I know," he said. "Tell 'em I've gone to South America. Tell 'em I've gone anywhere you can think of that's a long way off. I'm leaving town tonight and that's no joke. I sold Jean Wilson a bottle of the stuff, and her father's coming after me with a horse whip. I guess I'll go down to Madisonville and stay with Aunt Minnie till this blows over. But don't tell anybody that's where I'm going. And lend me all the money you've got."

"You owe me money," I said. "What about that ten percent commission?"

"I'll pay you when I get back," he said. "I have to finance a long trip now. How much you got?"

I dug up twelve dollars and eighty cents and gave it to him. He took it and ducked out the back door.

The telephone was still ringing so I answered it. It

was another girl.

"I want to speak to Bill Kinney," she said.

"Bill has just left on a business trip to South America," I said.

"I'll bet he has," she said.

"That's what he said," I said.

"He's a liar," she said.

"Bill is frequently a truthful boy," I said.

"I'm going to kill him," she said.

"You'll have to stand in line," I said, "There are a lot of girls ahead of you. In fact, one of them may have caught him already."

"I hope so," she said, "I'll help cut up the body." And she hung up.

I started up toward the front of the store, hoping to get away from the telephone before it rang again. The front door banged open and Elizabeth Hamilton came running in. Her hair was bright green and her face was bright red.

"Cary," she said, "is there a doctor around here? I've phoned all their offices and homes and I can't find one anywhere."

"All of the doctors have gone to the District Medical Convention over at Postoak City tonight," I said. "But don't worry about your hair, Elizabeth. You don't need a doctor for that; it'll wear off in a few days.

Of course, I didn't know whether it would wear off or not, but I could tell she was terribly agitated, so I thought I ought to calm her down as much as possible.

"It's not my hair that I'm worried about right now," she said. She was fidgeting from one foot to the other and squirming all over.

"What else is wrong?" I said.

"Cary," she said, "it's hard for me to tell you, but if I can't get a doctor, I've simply got to tell somebody. I can't stand this any longer." And she began to scratch in a funny place for a girl to scratch.

"You can tell me if you think I could be of any help to you," I said. "You see, I work with the doctors here at the drug-store and I'm familiar with the ethics of the medical profession."

"Cary," she said, "you know a girl has hair on another place besides her head. Well, I'm going to be married next month, so I thought when I got that stuff from Bill that it would be nice if *all* my hair was curly when I got married. So I put some of that awful stuff on the hair on the other place, too."

"That's all right," I said. "It'll wear off there, too. Especially after you get married."

"That isn't the point," she said, and she fidgeted worse than ever. "Some of the terrible stuff must have gotten *inside* down there. I tell you, Cary. I'm simply burning up down there. I want to scratch that place to pieces. I can't stand it." She jumped up and down like a little girl in the first grade who needs to go to the bathroom mighty bad.

I saw that it was pretty bad. I remembered something I had once heard Dr. Clinton prescribe for a woman who was having itching trouble in that spot.

"Elizabeth," I said, "you go home and put some ice cubes and two heaping tablespoonfuls of soda in a quart of water. Then soak a washcloth in that water and use it as a poultice down there. It'll stop the burning and itching."

"Cary," she said, "I can't possibly go home in this condition. I ran all the way down here, and it got worse every step. I think I would faint along the way if I tried to go back."

"Maybe we can do it here," I said. "You go back there in Mr. Gates' darkroom, and I'll bring the things you'll need."

I got some crushed ice from the soda fountain, put it

in a root beer stein, and added the soda and water. And then I got a fresh towel from the back bar and took all of the things back to Elizabeth.

"You can lie on this table," I said. "You should change the cloth every few minutes."

"Hurry up and get out of here so I can start," she said.

I got out and went back up to the front, wondering whether the treatment would do her any good or not. Some customers came in and I waited on them. The telephone rang some more and I answered it. I was afraid Mr. Brown would come back before I could get Elizabeth out of the darkroom. I didn't know what in the world I could tell him if he did.

About fifteen or twenty minutes had gone by when Elizabeth came walking up to the front. She was calm as a cucumber.

"That was wonderful," she said. "It not only stopped the burning and itching but it changed the color back again."

"You mean your hair isn't green anymore?" I said. "That *is* wonderful! That may save Bill's hide after all."

"No, it won't," she said. "I'm still going to kill him the first time I see him. But I do thank you for that treatment. I'm going home now and wash my hair in soda water."

"You won't have to put ice in it for that purpose," I said.

"I'd hope not," she said. She gave me back the root beer stein and the towel. "Don't ever tell anybody about this," she said as she went out the door.

"Don't worry," I said, "I'm just as interested in keeping this quiet as you are."

I started telephoning the other girls and telling them to wash their hair in soda water, that Bill had made a slight mistake in mixing the formula this time, and that he would be glad to refund their money as soon as he got back from South America.

Later one of the girls asked me how I found out that soda water would take out the green color.

"Serendipity," I said.

## Kiowa Crime Wave

Jesse James Weaver was on a big one. He had swigged a gallon of chock beer which he had bought from Charley Walters, plus maybe a little Jamaica Ginger he had wangled from Bill at the drug-store. He had whooped and hollered all night, and now he was down like a snake. He was lying on the courthouse lawn, foaming at the mouth, and holding on to the grass to keep from falling off.

"What's the matter with Jesse?" Hawkshaw Cummins, the city marshal, asked.

"He either went mad and bit hisself or bit hisself and went mad. I ain't certain which come first," Cats Killman, the night watchman, said.

"In either case, I reckon we'll have to shoot him to get him out of his misery," Hawkshaw said.

"I reckon we ort to," Cats said, "but ain't it kinder against the law?"

"I ain't no lawyer," Hawkshaw said, "but I am a good judge of what Jesse needs." He started to pull out his gun.

Maybe Jesse wasn't as drunk as he acted for he heard what Hawkshaw said. He jumped up and started running.

He ran through the crowd, across the square, and down the alley behind the stores.

"Why didn't you shoot him while you had the chance?" Cats said.

"I didn't aim to shoot him," Hawkshaw said. "I just wanted to scare him sober."

"You overdone it," Cats said, "Now we'll have to chase him."

They started after Jessie. He had a good start on them, but they knew were to look for him. They went down to Big Six's house.

When they got there Big Six was standing out on her front porch in her work clothes. That is, she was wearing a kimono and high-heeled bedroom slippers.

"You don't have to ask me," she said. "I know who you are looking for. Yes, he *was* here but he *ain't.*"

"What happened, Miz Watson?" Hawkshaw said.

"I don't have to put on no pretenses with you gentle-men," Big Six said. "Mostly I rape mighty easy, you might say, but I wasn't going to let Jesse James Weaver get away with anything like he tried on me. I hit him over the head with a stick o' stove wood. I didn't kill him but it wasn't because I didn't try to."

"You done good, Miz Watson," Hawkshaw said. "Better luck next time."

"Thank ya, Hawkshaw," Big Six said. "I try to be reasonable."

"Which away did he go?" Hawkshaw said.

"He went down towards the creek." Big Six said.

Hawkshaw and Cats headed toward the creek.

"She looked kinder wore out and painted over, didn't she?" Cats said.

"She's had a hard life," Hawkshaw said.

On the way to the creek they met Reuben Richards.

"Did you see Jesse James Weaver down this away?" Hawkshaw said.

"Yes, I seen him," Reuben said, "and I done more than seen him. I kicked his tail over a bob wire fence."

"Why did you do that?" Hawkshaw said.

"He tried to rob me, " Reuben said. "He played like he had a gun in his side coat pocket and tried to hold me up— like they do in the movies. I knowed he didn't have no gun in the first place; and I wasn't gonna let no squirt like Jesse James Weaver hold me up even if he did have a gun in the second place. So like I said, I just kicked his tail over the fence. He was still runnin' the las' time I seen him."

"Which away was he goin'?" Hawkshaw said.

"He seemed to be goin' on down the creek," Reuben said.

Hawkshaw and Cats turned down the creek.

"Maybe we can cut him off at the bridge," Cats said.

"He needs to be cut off somewhere besides the bridge," Hawkshaw said.

About that time they saw smoke coming up from behind Tom Toggle's shack, down between the creek and the railroad.

"Reckon Tom's house is afire?" Cats said.

"Looks like it might be," Hawkshaw said. "Maybe we better see about it."

They ran toward the house. Just then they heard Jesse James Weaver squawking like a game rooster. It sounded like he was down back of Tom's doggie shack. When they came around the corner of Tom's house, they saw a pretty sight. With one hand Tom Toggle was holding Jesse James Weaver by the neck of his coat and shaking him like a cat shaking a rat, and with the other hand he was pouring a bucket of water on a blazing brush pile. Jesse's head was still connected with his body but just barely.

"What's the matter, Tom?" Hawkshaw said.

"This dang fool tried by burn my house down," Tom said. "If I hadn't a caught him when I did, I'd be burned out of house and home by now. He was startin' a brush pile agin' the back of my house."

"Let me have him," Hawkshaw said. "You must be tired a shakin' him; let me do it a while."

"I ain't too tired to shake hell out of him a while longer," Tom said. "You pour water a while and then I can do a better job of shakin' him."

"I'll take over when you get tired," Hawkshaw said.

"I'd like a little of that, too." Cats said.

When Tom turned him loose, Jesse tried to run, but

Hawkshaw grabbed him.

"Looky here, Jesse," Hawkshaw said, "we already got you charged with public intoxication, attempted rape, attempted armed robbery, and arson. And now you're resistin' arrest. This could get serious, you know."

"Of course, I'm resistin' arrest," Jesse said. "I know if you ever get me in that stout house you'll lock the door and tie the key on a fast runnin' jackrabbit. I ain't takin' any chances."

"Don't kid yourself, Jesse," Hawkshaw said. "We ain't wastin' any good tax-payers' money on a polecat like you in jail. You go on home and sober up and behave yourself. We ain't goin' put up with you skylarkin' always."

He shoved Jesse halfway back to town.

"You let him go?" Cats said.

"Yeh," Hawkshaw said, "I'd say he's been punished right smart already — what with Big Six hittin' him over the head with a stick o' stove wood and Reuben Richards kickin' his tail over a bob wire fence and Tom here shakin' the livin' daylights out of him. And besides, if he was in jail, me and you wouldn't have anything to do around this town. We might even lose our jobs."

## The Midnight Ride of Skillet Woodburn
## (and the Big Oilman)

A big oilman was on a big deal. He had to deliver a certified check for $500,000 to the office of the Prairie Oil and Gas Company in the McCluskey Hotel in Ranger before midnight in order to sew it up. He thought it was worth at least another half-million dollars to him to get it nailed down that night. He got off the train from Fort Worth at 10:15 p.m., and it was 84 miles to Ranger. Skillet Woodburn met the train with his service car. The oilman told Skillet he would pay him $500 to get him to Ranger before midnight.

"Would you say that again?" Skillet said. (Skillet had never been more than nine dollars ahead of his creditors since he started driving a service car.)

"I need to get to Ranger before midnight," the oilman said, "I'll pay you five hundred dollars to get me there."

"Mister, just get in this auto," Skillet said.

"I have to get some papers signed first," the oilman said, "I'll be back in a minute."

He walked across the street to the Colonial Hotel, where two men met him. They signed the papers without even looking at them. The oilman came back to Skillet's car.

"I'm ready," he said.

Skillet stopped at the Tippett well out at the edge of town and filled the tank of his Model T Ford with casing-head gasoline. When he cranked it, the engine snorted like a racehorse, and Skillet had to climb over the hood into the front seat to keep from getting run over.

"When you put casing head gasoline in one of these things, it'll get you down and stomp you if you ain't careful," he explained to the oilman.

"Which is the best way to Ranger from here?" the oilman asked.

"There ain't no best way," Skillet said.

"There's bound to be a best way," the oilman said.

"I'm sorry there ain't," Skillet said. "The way by Carbon and Eastland may be the least worst, but there ain't no best way. If you go that way, you hit sand beds and ditches and if you go by Hogtown, you hit mud holes and broke-down bridges. You could just about flip a nickel. In fact, since you need to get to Ranger so bad, it would be better if you didn't have to start from here at all."

"I guess we'd better start anyway," the oilman said, "since we're here."

"That's what we're doin'," Skillet said, " but it's not my first choice. I'd rather start from Cisco."

The wind blew and the sand whipped against the windshield and Skillet stepped on the gas. The casing head gasoline began to take hold. The hoot owls in the post oaks hooted, and the screech owls in the mesquite trees screeched, and the Model T sang a song that might have fitted the Twilight of the Gods. Skillet stepped on the gas.

The oilman cowered in his corner of the seat and a team of jug-headed mules hitched to a wagon with a load of cotton in it got scared and ran away and scattered the cotton and the high wind spread it over parts of three counties and the farmer never did get much of it back and wanted to sue somebody but never could find out who did it but he still talked about it for years when he came to town on Saturday or First Monday to do his trading. Skillet stepped on the gas.

The radiator boiled and the left headlight went out and the engine began to knock like somebody was hitting the block with a sledgehammer. Skillet stepped on the gas

The front wheels hit a mud puddle and mud splattered the windshield and some of it came over the top and hit the oilman in the face. Skillet stepped on the gas.

All of a sudden the engine died and the car coasted three hundred yards down a long hill and stopped just like it never intended to start again. Skillet stepped on the gas but it didn't do any good.

"What's the matter with it?" the oilman asked.

"The wick in the taillight is probably a little low," Skillet said.

Skillet got out and took off the hood. Most of the engine block was red hot. He scooped up a hatful of water from a ditch and poured it into the radiator. Then he kicked the engine in the ribs. Then he spun the crank like a top. The engine started with a roar, and Skillet swung onto the running board as the car went by him. It went up the next hill faster than it had come down the last one. Just beyond the top of the hill the right front wheel hit a soft spot and the Model T lurched into a ditch. Skillet jerked it back onto the road and stepped on the gas.

The oilman seemed nervous. Skillet had heard Uncle Bailey Nabors tell about how old-time cowboys sang to the cattle on a stormy night to soothe their nerves. He decided to sing to the oilman. He sang:

"Rocks on the mountain and fish in the sea;

O, a blond-headed woman made a fool outa me!"

But he didn't stop stepping on the gas while he sang. He just finished one song and started another one.

"And when I die don't bury me a tall;

Just pickle my bones in alkyhol.

Put a bottle of booze at my head and feet;

And then I'll know that my bones will keep.

Put a Camel Cigarette In the corner of my mouth,

So the people will know that my light's gone out."

A big bulldog ran out from a farmhouse and chased along by the side of the car barking like crazy. Skillet held the steering wheel with one hand and reached over and grabbed the dog by the collar with his other hand. Just as he took a left turn, he heaved the dog into the backseat of the car. That was the surprisedest dog in seven states! He lay there on the backseat and cried like a baby. Skillet hit him over the head with his hat now and then and hauled him ten miles and then threw him out into a creek. That dog didn't chase the car anymore.

Five thousand miles (roughly) to the northeast, President Woodrow Wilson was beginning another nerve wracking day at the Paris Peace Conference. Elderly empires were passing out of existence and infant republics were struggling to be born. Skillet stepped on the gas.

"How old are you?" the oilman asked.

"I'm seventeen," Skillet said.

"So you're still in school?"

"No, I'm outa school."

"You've already graduated from high school at seventeen?"

"No, I reckon I quituated."

"That's too bad."

"Well, I had a little encouragement to quit. I sorta scared one of the teachers."

"How did that happen?"

"Well, I took the honkin' part out of one of them old-fashioned honkers on a car. You remember the kind where you squeezed a rubber bulb and the horn honked? Well, the part that actually done the honkin' was only two or three inches long. I took it out and wrapped it in my handkerchief and took it up to school. We had a little Domestic Science teacher named Miss

Wray. She was pretty as a picture but she was excitable. I didn't take Domestic Science, of course, but she kept one of the study halls I was in. I was sittin' right behind her desk. I took out my handkerchief and pretended to blow my nose, but I blew that Model T honker instead. It made an awful racket. Miss Wray jumped over her desk and fainted. And when the Principal picked her up, there was a wet spot on the floor. They sorta encouraged me to quit school after that."

Up to this point, as Skillet saw it, the trip had been routine, almost humdrum. But then something special happened. Before you could say Jim Ferguson right fast, without any warning whatever, a pillar of fire 200 feet high roared up into the night sky and lighted up the whole countryside for miles and miles. This geyser of flame was followed by a long dull roar that was earth shaking. Skillet had a fleeting feeling that it was the end of the world. Something of gigantic proportions was happening and Skillet didn't crave the role of happenee. For a split second he let up on the gas.

"What do you reckon that was?" he asked the oilman.

The oilman knew about such things.

"I'd say that a well has just blown in and caught fire. A wildcat and the tool  dresser probably had his forge going right under the derrick. It must the Duke No. 1, over toward Hogtown. If I didn't need to get to Ranger so bad, I'd go over there and start buying some leases."

"But you still want to go to Ranger?" Skillet said.

"Yes, I guess I'll have to, but I surely hate to pass up a chance like this."

Skillet floorboarded it again.

The pillar of flame subsided somewhat, Skillet snaked the Model T Through three sand beds, the other headlight went out, and he steered by the swish-swish of the fence posts on each side of the road. The oilman showed signs of heart failure, but then they saw the lights of Ranger.

But right at the edge of town they ran into trouble. A roadblock made out of oil drums closed the street, and a deputy sheriff with a flashlight was standing at each end of it. It seemed like the farmer who owned the purloined bulldog had telephoned in that a crazy man was driving along the road at ninety miles an hour, endangering life and property, and stealing dogs. So the deputies had set up the roadblock to stop him. Skillet rawhided his mount to a halt just shy of the barrels. The oilman groaned.

"You're under arrest for speedin', reckless drivin', stealin' a dog, and drivin' without lights," one of the deputies said.

"That's right," Skillet said, "I'm glad you gentlemen called it to my attention. Have you heard about the Duke well? It just blew in at about 10,000 barrels a day and lots of gas pressure. It opens up a whole new field. But before the people here find out about it, you ought to be able to pick up some leases close to it pretty cheap."

"Was that what caused the fire and the explosion down that way while ago?" one of the deputies asked.

"Yes, it was," Skillet said.

"Come on," the other deputy said. "What're we foolin' around here for?" The two deputies ran and jumped into their car.

Skillet kicked two of the oil drums out of the way and drove through the gap. At 11:45 he pulled up in front of the McCluskey Hotel.

"I thought we were goin' to run out of gas in that last sand bed," Skillet said.

The oilman seemed relieved. He counted out $500 in $20 bills and gave them to Skillet.

"Thank you," Skillet said, "I sure have enjoyed this."

P.S. Skillet took the $500 and made a down payment on a Hudson Super-Six touring car. Then he could drive from Kiowa to Ranger in an hour and a half without hurrying so much.

# Delirium

The influenza epidemic kept on. It was the big one that came after the First World War, you know. The doctors were out all day and all night, and people were dying all over the county, including two boys in my high school class. One morning at the drug-store my face got to feeling hotter and hotter and I ached all over.

"I'm afraid I'm sick," I told Mr. Brown.

"Take a couple of aspirin tablets," he said. "We've got to wait on these people."

I took the aspirin tablets. After a while I felt a little better. And I kept on working — all that day and until ten o'clock that night. By that time I was shaky and didn't have very good sense. I walked home in a cold rain and went to bed. I was cold on the outside and hot on the inside.

Some time in the night Dr. Clinton came after me and took me up to the drug-store to get some ether for him. By the time I got in bed again I didn't know which one of the boys I was. I thought I was still at the drug-store waiting on people. Sometimes I could see them and sometimes I couldn't see them but could hear them. They got all mixed up together. I couldn't always tell who said what. It went sort of like this:

"Was he drunk?"
"No, he wasn't drunk."
"How do you know he wasn't drunk?"
"I kicked him and he moved."

~ ~ ~

"Where's Jesse?"
"They've got him where the cold wind won't blow on him now."

"You mean he's in the stout house?"
"I mean he's gettin' free board in a rock hotel."

~  ~  ~

"Is her stuff good?"
"Well, it's better'n a knothole."

~  ~  ~

"Like they told us in the army, when you get there, there'll be somebody there to carry your luggage, and that'll be you."

~  ~  ~

"My trouble is that I've got too much business for one clerk and not enough for two."

~  ~  ~

"The way things are in this country now, the future's a thing of the past."

~  ~  ~

"I haven't done much thinkin' lately; it's been too hot and dry; but I aim to start again this fall after we've had a rain and the weather gets cool."

~  ~  ~

"How's your cotton-pickin' comin' along?"
"Purty good; we've got one bale out and forty acres on the second one."

~  ~  ~

"Joe Bailey is the best public speaker I've ever heard."
"He uses them three cornered words and he makes 'em fit together."

~  ~  ~

"Luther, you're so awkward that if you had horns you'd hook yourself."

~ ~ ~

"Where're your boys now, Uncle George?"
"Hoke's in South Texas stealin' sheep, and Gaston's preachin' to keep him out of hell."

~ ~ ~

"Hack to Hogtown — ladies only."

~ ~ ~

"Just got a letter from old Doc Darnicky — said to crate her up and ship her back to Hipperdonia — she ain't what we ordered."

~ ~ ~

"Doc's been dead for years. He's just too mean to lay down."

~ ~ ~

"That boy's tough as a boot and twice as high."

~ ~ ~

"Whata ya say, Jesse?"
"Save ya bottles, boys, it may rain booze."

~ ~ ~

"Are ya travelin' or goin' somewhere?"
"I reckon not either one. We're just cotton-pickers goin' through the country lookin' for work."

~ ~ ~

"I'd rather be poor and work for a livin' than to pick cotton."

~ ~ ~

"Where'd ya get that car?"
"I borrowed it."
"What did the owner say?"
"He wasn't at home."

~ ~ ~

"I saw ol' Pat Brannigan settin' on his front porch barefooted while ago."
"Yeh, he ain't proud. He don't care who sees his feet."

~ ~ ~

"A corporation is an artificial person, invisible, intangible, and existing only in the contemplation of the law—having neither tail to be kicked nor soul to damned."

~ ~ ~

"I ain't sayin' you ain't right; but if you wasn't so damn much bigger than me, you'd be wrong as hell."

~ ~ ~

"Gimme a sody."
"What flavor?"
"Red."

~ ~ ~

"I don't have to talk sweet to you. I'm not running for office and I don't owe you any money."

~ ~ ~

"Yes, old Abe Slocum lived to be 107, but whiskey and chewin' tobacco finally killed him."

~ ~ ~

"Yes, her name is Tarzeen. You see, her daddy wanted a boy and was going to name him Tarzan. But she turned out to be a girl instead of a boy, so we named her Tarzeen. And I reckon she has lived up to it pretty well. She can climb a tree better than most boys can, and I have an awful time keeping decent clothes on her. She's a tomboy all right."

~ ~ ~

"You say Janey Stokes got married to Ed Tutwiler."
"Yeh, that's right."
"The pore girl must a wanted to go to a weddin' mighty bad."

~ ~ ~

"Yes, I was raised in Arkansas, but them that could read come to Texas."

~ ~ ~

"My daddy died when I was nine years old, so with me it was a case of 'root, hog or die pore'."

~ ~ ~

"Is he honest?"
"Well, he's honest if you watch him close enough."

~ ~ ~

"Kiowa don't seem to grow very fast, does it?"
"No, every time a baby is born, a young man leaves town."

~ ~ ~

"How much did the baby weigh when it was born?"
"Four pounds and seven ounces."
"That's mighty small, isn't it?"
"Yes, it's so dry here in West Texas you do well to

get your seed back."

~  ~  ~

"Whata ya aimin' to do now that you're outa the pen?"

"I've decided to earn a honest livin'."

"Well, you won't have no competition in that field of endeavor in this town."

~  ~  ~

"Is there a toilet in this building?"

"No ma'm; I'm sorry there isn't. The nearest one is in the basement over at the courthouse."

"Come on quick, junior."

~  ~  ~

"You can't tell me nothin' about *class*. I've delivered ice in the best houses in this town."

"You haven't got anything on me. I've delivered groceries in the same houses where you delivered ice."

~  ~  ~

"I've been barberin' for ten years now, and I'm gettin' mighty tired of scrapin' chins. I've got a little money saved up, and I'm thinkin' serious about goin' to dental college. I'd like to be a dentist. What do you think about it, Uncle George?"

"Well, Ethan, I think you ought to go ahead and do it. You *already* know how to work the chair."

~  ~  ~

"Local option prohibition was voted in here in Kiowa in 1904. Before that there was a saloon on every side of the square."

"That means that by 1904 the Baptists and the Methodists outnumbered the rest of the people here?"

"Well, they was some Campbellites, too."
~ ~ ~

"Oh throw me in that dungeon;
Oh, throw me in that cell;
Oh, put me where the north wind blows
From the southwest side of hell."
~ ~ ~

"Are you married?"
"Well, not often nor for long at a time."
~ ~ ~

"He used to teach school here, didn't he?"
"Yes, he was principal of the grammar school when I went there."
"Was he a good disciplinarian?"
"When he said 'frog' the boys jumped first, and then asked 'how high?' while they were on the way up."
~ ~ ~

"Tiny Tutwiler is six feet seven inches tall and weighs 290 pounds."
"Why do you call him Tiny?"
"He likes for us to call him that, and we don't want to displease him."
~ ~ ~

"All that can save this country now is the Ku Klux Klan. If the Klan candidates don't get elected, I'm movin' to Mexico."
"If the Klan candidates *do* get elected, I'll carry you as far as Laredo."
~ ~ ~

"I'll cut you so low you'll need a stepladder to see

over a dime."

~ ~ ~

"Tell another one to prop that one up."

~ ~ ~

"Do you think you'll ever pay for your raising?"
"I don't know— I'm not gettin' much."

~ ~ ~

"How ya feel?"
"Like I'd been sent for and couldn't come."

~ ~ ~

"Hell's afloat and the river's risin'."

~ ~ ~

"Them eyes, them eyes; them's what rurn't me."

~ ~ ~

"I ain't a gonna vote for nobody for nothin' less the price of cotton goes up."

~ ~ ~

"If Obidiah's ever sinned, they've been sins of o-mission and not commission, because Obidiah don't commit. What I mean, he don't never do nothin'."

~ ~ ~

"How come you come?"
"I reckon I come to see and to be seen."

~ ~ ~

"What did they ever do to that feller?"
"Which one was that?"
"The one that got mixed up in the doin's down

yonder?”

"O him? They never could prove nothin' on him."

"That's exactly the way I figured it would turn out."

"You was right."

~ ~ ~

"We're gonna put the little pot in the big one, fry the skillet, and throw away the lid."

"You mean you're gonna kill a big one."

"I mean it's gonna be like the night of the royal castration; we're gonna remove the king's final ball."

~ ~ ~

"Here's to you, you deaf old son-of-a-bitch."

"The same back at you."

~ ~ ~

"Jesse, you shore do tell it scary."

~ ~ ~

"They all live in the immediate vicinity around here."

"What do you mean by the immediate vicinity?"

"In West Texas, the immediate vicinity extends as far as two men can ride fast in as many days as it takes them to get there."

~ ~ ~

"Did you know John Butler."

"I wouldn't a knowed him from Adam's off ox."

~ ~ ~

"I'll do it for you if you want me to, but it'll be a West Texas job."

~ ~ ~

"They are some boys in this town — like Gabe Hopson and Joe Bollen—that don't care what the Lord thinks about 'em — much less what the preachers think about 'em. They ain't so mean; they just don't want anybody tellin' 'em what to do."

~ ~ ~

"Thirty years ago this county was all cattle ranchin', with maybe a few sheep here and there. But since then a lot of cotton farmers have moved in. Only two or three of the big ranches are left. We've got cotton and cotton gins all over the place now."

~ ~ ~

"John Butler wasn't the kind of man who would have gone to hell for a dime, but he might have fooled around the hole till he fell in."

~ ~ ~

"You know our ancestors must a been hot-tempered people to a fought for a country like this."

~ ~ ~

"If you'd pull up your pants and get a haircut, you might get elected."

~ ~ ~

"They've put him where the dogs won't bite him now."

"You mean in the pen."

"I mean in the pen — for five years."

"I reckon he'll have right smart time to figure out whether he ought to a done it or not."

"I reckon he will, if he hasn't already made up his mind about it."

~ ~ ~

"Hode was ridin' one of Wes Hardin's racehorses. It turned out to be bad judgment, because he nearly caught up with Wes. When Hode got within about fifty yards of him, Wes turned around in his saddle and shot at him with his six-shooter. It was too long range for a pistol shot, but it nearly scared Hode to death. When we caught up with him, he was pullin' the bits down that racehorse's throat to keep him from goin' so fast."

~ ~ ~

"Is Tom F. goin' to get elected?"
"I don't know, but he's runnin' like a skeered wolf."

~ ~ ~

"It was a military wedding, you know. The groom was escorted to the altar by the bride's father — with a shotgun."

~ ~ ~

"If that's the way you've been behavin', maybe we better send your name in for prayer."

~ ~ ~

"I understand that there's precedent for immaculate conception, but I think there's room for reasonable doubt about it in Cuba Stokes's case."

~ ~ ~

I didn't get out of bed for three weeks. I had influenza, of course, but then it turned into pneumonia. They said I nearly died the second week, but that first night was the worst. I reckon I was delirious.

## The Old McClean House

Yes, people *talk* a lot about the old McClean house, but they don't really *know* much about it. It's for sure that old Mr. McClean was killed there, but it's not by any means certain who killed him. Somebody shot him with a pistol that summer night. Everybody agreed on that, but that's where the agreement ended.

I was just a small boy when it happened — about ten years old, I reckon.

You see, old Mr. McClean's only son, Kermit, was living with him. I mean Kermit was married and he and his wife lived there in the big house with old Mr. McClean. You see, old Mr. McClean's wife was dead and had been dead for years, maybe twenty years or so. She died when Kermit was just a very small boy. So old Mr. McClean was a widower who had lived by himself for all those years until Kermit and his wife came back to Kiowa to live with him. Yes, Kermit came back and worked at the bank with his father.

Now Kermit's wife was a woman for you and then some. She wasn't a Kiowa girl; Kermit had married her way back East somewhere, just after he got out of college (He went to Harvard, you know the only boy from Kiowa that has ever done that.) Well, this girl he married was built from the ground up, what the young fellows these times call "really stacked". You've seen Babe O'Hara around here the last few years with her twerky twat and her legs looking like they were just intended to make a man hungry? Well, she kinda reminds me of Kermit McClean's wife only she hasn't got as much of what it takes. This town hasn't ever seen many, if any, like her, and I don't reckon it ever will. They made her and then they broke the mold.

When she walked downtown the boys that hung out around the barbershop would start watching her as soon as she turned the corner of the square and they would keep it up till she went out of sight around the post office corner. That gave them two full blocks and three street crossings, and they always made the most of the whole distance. It took the place of movies, television, and paperbacks for them.

But to get back to that summer night when old Mr. Mac was killed. It was pouring down rain that night, a regular gully-washer and fence-lifter. Maybe even a toad-drownder, as they say back in East Texas. Most of the time, you know, it's hot and dry here in the summertime, but sometimes it *does* rain in the summertime and when it does, it's apt to be a hooper-dooper. Well, it was that night. The big mesquite trees up on the hill by the reservoir nearly bent double in the wind. Great claps of thunder bounced the clouds around and except when there was a flash of lightning, it was as dark as a stack of black cats.

I was walking home from the picture show and since I was already as wet as a drowned rat, there wasn't any use hurrying any more. So I was just walking along slow under the big trees that hung over the sidewalk at the side of the old McClean house. I heard a pistol shot and I'm sure that it was the one that killed Mr. McClean. I was scared and I stopped and looked toward the house. There wasn't any streetlights in Kiowa in those days, so I couldn't see a thing until there was a flash of lightning. Then the flash was gone and I couldn't see any more.

Well, naturally there was a big to-do when the richest man in town gets shot in his own bedroom. The sheriff and the constable and the city marshal all came — along with about half the rest of the people in town — and they looked around and asked questions and tried to find out what had happened. Old Mr. Mac was plumb dead — a .45 bullet straight through his head —

so he couldn't tell anybody anything. Kermit and his wife both said they were in their own bedroom upstairs when they heard the shot. They ran down, they said, but whoever had done it was already gone. Mr. McClean, they said, was already dead on the floor when they got there and whoever had shot him must have jumped out the window.

They reckoned it was a burglar come to rob him because everybody knew he was a rich banker and might have a lot of money on him (There never had been a burglary in Kiowa, but there has to be a first time for anything.)

Or maybe, Kermit said, it was a cattleman or a cotton farmer that the bank had foreclosed on and was mad at old Mr. Mac for doing it. (He had made what you might call a success of foreclosing on mortgages, especially during the big drought.)

Or maybe, Kermit added, it was just somebody who had a grudge against him for something he had done a long time ago (You see Mr. Mac had been mixed up in the John Wesley Hardin doin's when he was a young man way back in the 1870's.)

And that was all that the sheriff and the constable and the city marshal and the county attorney and the district attorney and the coroner could ever get out of Kermit and his wife.

Kermit even hired a private detective from Fort Worth to come out and investigate the case. But he couldn't find much either. He looked for tracks under the window, but, of course, the rain had washed them away. He looked for the pistol too and finally found one out in the yard, but it turned out to be one that belonged to old Mr. Mac himself, one that he had had for years and years, an old thumb-buster Colt .45. The detective talked about looking for fingerprints on it — that was a new fangled thing then — but after it had laid out in the rain all that night, he couldn't find anything on it but a lot of mud. So the detective gave up, Kermit paid him, and he went back to Fort Worth.

Gradually people stopped talking about the murder all the time, and started talking about Woodrow Wilson and William Howard Taft and Teddy Roosevelt again. In a few months Kermit and his wife closed up the big house, sold the bank, and moved to Dallas. Nobody has ever lived in the old house since then.

After a while people began to say the house was haunted. You know how things like that get started. People like to have something to scare theirselves with, I reckon. That house isn't anymore haunted than I am, but you could probably find a hundred people in this town who would swear on a stack of bibles as high as the courthouse that they have seen and heard things there that prove it *is* haunted.

After the excitement was sorta over, I began to remember some things. I remembered hearing men who were old-timers in Kiowa — like Uncle George Hobart and Hode Barnes — say that old Mr. Mac had been a genuwine hell-raiser with women when he was a young man. I wouldn't know about that first hand, of course — it was too long before my time.

But I did know some things that I had seen for myself. I remembered seeing him take Kermit's wife out for a ride in his big Hupmobile, late in the evenings, many times, when Kermit was gone, as he often was — maybe over to Post Oak City to get some papers signed for the bank or something like that. They would start from the big house on the hill and drive out into the country, and it would be after dark when they got back.

And one time when Homer Dunlap and me were walking back pretty late from fishing way down below the railroad bridge on Kiowa Creek, we saw the big Hupmobile parked where the road swung in near the creek, and Mr. Mac and his daughter-in-law were down at the creek. She had her shoes and stockings off and her skirt rolled up and was wading in the shallow water at the edge of the creek. And he was throwing little rocks into the creek and making the water splash up on her bare legs. Every time her legs got splashed, she would squeal and he would laugh. They were having so much fun with each other that they didn't see Homer and me at all. We hid behind some bushes and watched them.

After a while she stepped on a slick rock and fell down into the water. She screamed and he laughed louder than ever.

"You're going to have to take off your clothes and dry them before we can go back to town," Mr. Mac said.

"Not with you around," She said, "We aren't going *that* far."

"If you don't take them off, I'll have to take them off for you," he said.

"Just you try it," she said. Then she ran over toward a thicket and he ran after her.

Homer was the Sunday School kind of boy and he was scared. I was a little disturbed too.

"We better leave," he said.

"Yes, I reckon we had," I said.

All of this came back to my mind when I had time to do some quiet remembering.

Now the point is that when that flash of lightning came just after I heard the pistol shot that I saw somebody jump out the window. I was a kid only about ten years old, and I hadn't ever seen a naked woman before in my life, but I knew immediately and absolutely that the person I saw jump out of that window was a naked woman, and a mighty well built naked woman at that.

So maybe it was Kermit's wife that shot old Mr. Mac,

but if it happened that way, she may have had a good reason for doing it.

Or maybe Kermit surprised them together and shot him. If it happened that way, maybe Kermit had a good reason, too.

Or maybe when he got caught, old Mr. Mac shot himself and if it did happen that way, I'd say he had a good reason.

Anyway, I haven't ever told a soul about this before and I wouldn't be telling you now except you have always impressed me as being a gentleman and a scholar—and a judge of good whiskey — that knows enough to keep his mouth shut about things like this — and maybe this whiskey that you're a good judge of has had something to do with it, too. Anyway, Kermit and his wife are both dead now, and they never did have any children — in fact, there isn't a McClean left alive in the world so far as I know — so I reckon it couldn't hurt anybody now.

# The Plow

Bill and I were hunting quail in an old field. The field was near my Uncle Robert's farm out northwest of Kiowa. We had the weekend after Thanksgiving off from school and we were making the most of it. The field hadn't been cultivated for many years, so it had grown up in weeds, bull nettles, shin-oak bushes, and grass burrs. There were rabbits and armadillos and we hoped there were some bobwhites. We didn't have a dog, however, so we weren't having much luck.

Over beyond the edge of the field was an old house. All of the windows were broken out and the roof sagged between the two chimneys. The well had caved in and the barn was leaning against a big tree. You could tell that nobody had lived there in a long time. It was sort of creepy.

Just about in the middle of the field, we came across a plow. It was an old turning plow and the share was riddled with rust. The strangest part of it was that a set of mule harnesses was hanging on each of the plow handles. The leather was almost rotted away in places and the metal parts were all rusted. Bill touched one of the old collars and the stuffing began to pour out.

"Maybe we oughtn't to do that," I said.

"Maybe we oughtn't," Bill agreed, and he tried to stop up the hole. "What do you suppose happened here?"

"It looks like somebody was plowing and decided to stop."

If you looked closely you could see that the plow was standing at the end of the last furrow that had ever been plowed in that field.

"He not only stopped, he stopped for good it looks like."

"But why did he leave the harness?"

"Maybe he died — died right suddenly."

"Why didn't his son or one of the neighbors come after it?"

"I don't know. What do you think we ought to do about this?"

"Nothing—just nothing. It looks like that's what everybody else has been doing about it. That's what Colonel Brandon calls a 'precedent', and you're supposed to abide by a 'precedent'."

We walked off and started hunting quail again.

That night after supper I asked Uncle Robert about the plow. He sort of laughed and leaned back in his rocking chair.

"That plow has quite a story to it," he said. "I'm not sure I know all of it."

"Tell us what you do know."

"I reckon I do know enough to make it interesting and I can sorta guess at the rest of it. That old field you boys wandered into was part of Ham McCurdey's place. When I first knew Ham he was a young buck running around the country, chasing the girls, going to dances, and sort of raising hell generally."

"Robert, you oughtn't to use language like that before these young boys," Aunt Margaret said.

"That's right, I shouldn't," he agreed. He never disagreed with his wife.

"But one summer they had what we used to call a 'protracted meeting' at Sweetwater Church — or rather under the brush arbor near the church. Levi Tutwiler was doing the preaching. Levi was kinda a travelling preacher—didn't belong to any particular denomination that I ever heard of —just went around the country in the summertime preaching hell-fire and damnation wherever he could get anybody to listen to him. He had a wife and ten or twelve children, so they made a pretty good sized congregation whether anybody else showed up or not. He also had his unmarried younger sister, Mattie May Tutwiler, along with him and she played the organ.

"The first night Ham came to the meeting, he and some of the other boys sat back on the back row of the benches. But even from there, he could see Mattie May at the organ well enough to tell that she was a mighty pretty girl. The next night he was up on the front row and helping with the singing. He had a good whiskey-tenor voice, and he made a showing with Mattie May in a hurry.

"The upshot of it was that Ham fell in love and got converted all at one fell swoop, as they used to say. He followed the Tutwiler outfit all over Kiowa County that summer, and in the fall him and Mattie May got married. Ham was reborn. Made over. A changed man.

"He bought a quarter section of leftover sandy land, cleared it of post oaks, blackjacks, stretch-briars and prickly pears, built a plank house with two chimneys, sodded a Bermuda grass pasture, dug a 90 foot well, set out a peach orchard, put up bob-wire fences, irrigated a big vegetable garden, filled up the gullies, and paid off the mortgage — all in ten years.

"What I mean, he worked morning, noon, and night, and he never spent a cent of money on himself. Come to think about it, there probably wasn't any left to spend on himself, because he had Levi Tutwiler's family to support about half the time. Levi would take 'em off preaching during the summer, but as soon as it began to get cold in the fall, they'd all come traipsing back and live off of Ham during the winter and spring.

"And what's more, Mattie May would go off with them on all the preaching trips. I reckon she loved Ham some, but she loved playing that organ at the camp meetings better than anything. She would really bang it out when she got the spirit. So every summer Ham was

left to batch it by himself—and do all of the work —
while the rest of them were off bringing poor lost souls
to the Lord under the brush arbors.

"Ham and Mattie May never did have any children. I
don't know whether it was because she *couldn't* or she
*wouldn't*, but anyway she *didn't*."

"Robert, you oughtn't to talk about things like that
before these young boys," Aunt Margaret said.

"That's right, I oughtn't," he said.

"You boys aren't old enough to remember the oil
boom we had in this part of the country around the
time of the First World War. The biggest part of it was
around Ranger up in Eastland County, but there was a
lot of drilling here in Kiowa County, too. Some
wildcatters got some leases together right around here,
including Ham's place and mine and several others, and
they drilled the first hole over there in Ham's pasture.

"They started in the fall and piddled along all
through the winter. The tools would break down or
they would run out of money or something else would
go wrong. We had all just about run out of confidence
and patience with them because they never seemed to
get anywhere. But one morning along in the spring I
was plowing over in that south field of mine next to
Ham's place, and I heard sort of an explosion and then a
big roaring like a strong wind, and it all just plain
scared me. I started running over toward Ham's field
— yes, I could still run in those days — and I saw Ham
out in the middle of the field plowing.

"About the same time I saw one of the men from the
oilrig running toward Ham from the other direction.
Him and me got there about the same time.

"You've got a gusher," the oilman yelled above the
noise.

"How's that?" Ham asked.

"You've got a gusher — a well that's flowing about a

thousand barrels a day — lots of gas pressure!" the oilman told him again.

"Are you shore?" Ham asked him.

"Sure as hell! You can see it from here if you'll look."

"Ham took a good look. 'Maybe you better get back to it,' he said to the oilman."

"'Uncle Bob, will you excuse me?' he said to me. 'It looks like I've got some things to look after.'

"'Sure, Ham,' I said.

"He unhooked his mules from the plow and hung the harness on the plow handles. He did it slow like and gentle. And then he swung up on one of mules and rode him back to the barn. Other times he walked, but this time he rode.

"Well, the upshot of it was that Ham sold his land outright to the Prairie Oil and Gas Company for $150,000. If he had been experienced in such matters he probably could have got a good deal more, but they offered him $150,000 and since that sounded like all the money in the world to him, he took it and never looked back. As it turned out, it wasn't too bad a deal. The pool they had struck was shallow and the gas pressure played out in a few months. They pumped some of the wells for two or three years, but during the Depression they abandoned the whole thing. Since then they've even moved all of the old derricks and tanks. Now you can't tell the oil boom ever happened.

"They gave Ham a check on one of the big banks in Fort Worth and Ham got on the train at Kiowa — the old Frisco—and went to Fort Worth and cashed it. He brought the money back in a shoebox all in hundred dollar bills. He asked me to come over to his house to witness what he was going to do with it.

"He counted it out in three stacks — fifty thousand in each stack. He gave the first stack to Mattie May.

" 'Take this and do whatever you want to with it, so

long as I don't ever see you again.'

"He gave the next stack to Levi Tutwiler. 'This is for the Lord's work, which I guess will have to include your family. And I don't crave to see any more of any of you either.' He kept the last stack for himself.

"When him and me came out onto his front gallery, one of the oilmen drove up and got out.

" 'I have some papers here for you to sign, Mr. McCurdy,' he said.

" 'Now that I've got the money, I'll sign anything you say,' Ham said. He signed a lot of things.

"When the oilman was about to leave, he said, 'By the way, Mr. McCurdy, what about that plow you left out in the field? We'll probably start drilling there pretty soon.'

"'If you don't mind,' Ham said, 'I'd like to leave that there as a kind of a monument — a monument to ten long, hard, misspent years.'

" 'That's all right with us; we'll work around it.'

"So as you boys saw this afternoon, it's still there," Uncle Robert concluded.

~ ~ ~

"What became of all those people?" I asked.

"Well, Mattie May bought her a new house in De Leon and a new piano to go in it. Her neighbors said she played it morning, noon and night the year 'round. Later she got a job playing the piano at the picture show. I reckon she was happy.

"Levi Tutwiler seemed to lose interest in working for the Lord. He bought out an insurance agency in Cisco. Maybe his experience peddling hell-fire and brimstone helped him in selling insurance policies to people. He did fairly well.

"Ham took his money and went out to Lubbock and

developed a good, irrigated cotton farm. He's been
dead a number of years now — died young of a heart
attack."

## The Nicest Thing He Could A Done For Her

"Yes, I remember you — remember you well. But it *has* been a long time since I seen you last. You must a been gone from here something like twenty-five years, haven't you? Yes, I thought it was something like that. Anyway, it's good to see you again.

"Yes, I remember Grady Meachems, too. I'm kinda sorry you asked about him, though. He didn't turn out too well, I have to say. His father was a big cotton buyer, you remember, in the old days. Right well fixed at one time maybe one of the wealthiest men in town. But cotton-buying went all to hell in this part of the country after the First World War, you know.

"Cotton-buying was kinda a funny thing, you know. In the old days when Kiowa County used to produce over a hundred thousand bales of cotton a year, there musta been twenty-five or thirty cotton-buyers in this town. But after the boll weevil hit and the sandy-land farmers started raisin' peanuts, cotton production went down to only a few thousand bales a year. But none of the cotton-buyers quit bein' cotton- buyers. A few of them died, of course, but their sons usually taken over in their place. So this meant that there was too many cotton-buyers and too little cotton for them to buy. There was something sorta funny about it. I reckon the fact that a cotton-buyer didn't have to work more than three of four months outa the year had something to do with it. And it was respectable. You could be a cotton-buyer, not ever pay all your bills at any one time, and still stand good in the community. At least a lot of 'em tried it that way, and Old Man Meachems was one of 'em.

"But I reckon there has to be an end to all good things. He died and his creditors swooped down on his estate. That is, they tried to. But it turned out he hadn't left enough of an estate to wad a shotgun. Everything he had owned was mortgaged up to the eyebrows and then some.

"This left Grady in a mighty tight spot. Meantime, he had married Dorothy Eden. You remember her, I'm sure. She was Old Man Frank Eden's youngest daughter. He was president of the First National Bank and owned a lot of property around town and over the county. Dorothy went to Miss Hockaday's School in Dallas for a year or two after she graduated from high school here and then come home and married Grady. It was about the biggest weddin' Kiowa ever seen, I reckon.

"Even while his dad was still alive, Grady didn't do any too well. He pretended to be a cotton-buyer, but he didn't do enough business to grease a gimlet. Dorothy run up big bills at Higginbotham's and other stores around town, and Grady done the same. But after his father's death and the Big Depression come on, things really went bad. Old Man Eden kinda bailed him out a time or two — paid me a big bill he had run up here at my station. (Yeh, I was here even then—just lease it from Joe Turpin.) But purty soon after the Depression struck, Mr. Eden's bank failed, and he lost everything he had. That meant Grady was teetotally on his own, and that own was mighty scatterin'. Mainly he just sat in the shade on the east side of the Masonic Temple and waited for something to happen. Also he got drunk whenever he could gin-swiggle a boot-legger out of a bottle of liquor.

"Dorothy quit him and went off to Dallas and later got a divorce. I don't know what has ever become of her. Grady got down to where he was sleepin' in Joe Tilden's old livery stable and livin' on hamburgers. Joe would let him drive one of his service cars now and then, so he made enough to kinda keep soul and body together, but he was skinny as a snake and looked like the devil was only two jumps behind him.

"And then all of a sudden he had a big piece of luck. He met the train from Fort Worth one night in his service car and picked up a young woman who wanted to go up to the Ridgeway Hotel. She was a big blonde girl — kinda purty if there hadn't been so much of her — and she liked to talk. So did Grady, so they got to talkin' on the way from the depot up to the hotel. Grady could be plumb charmin' even when he was half drunk, and she evidently took a likin' to him from the very first. Turned out she had come to Kiowa from a little town in East Texas to take a job as head cook at the Ridgeway Hotel. Name was Irma Ratliff. I got to know her pretty well in later times, and I can tell you that she was just the kind of woman who was born to take care of some good-for-nothin' man. And Grady filled the bill plumb perfect.

"And that's what she done for him. She took him in like you might take in a sick puppy that didn't have no home. She fed him in the kitchen at the hotel, got a little room for him just off the kitchen, and made him stop drinkin'. He gained some weight and purty soon he was lookin' sorta like his old self.

"And maybe most important of all, she got him a job. I don't know how she done it, but somehow she got him a job workin' for the State Highway Department — drivin' a road grader and that kinda thing. The exercise and the fresh air was good for him, and he liked to drive anything that would run. He even paid off some of his debts and saved a little money.

"And then to top it off, they got married. I reckon she had been sweetheart, wife, nurse, mother, and general caretaker for him from the first. But anyway they made it all legal.

"Well sir, it looked like she had resurrected him for sure, but it was too good to last. I reckon makin' a man outa Grady Meachems was too big a job even for Irma Ratliff. After all, the Lord Himself had kinda botched the job, looks like.

"One Saturday in the fall, we had a big football game here. Kiowa was playin' Ranger for the District Championship, as I remember it, and Babe O'Hara came back from Fort Worth for the game. I don't know whether you ever knew Babe or not — she was probably too young for you — but anyway she was one of the worst cases of big tits and hot pants that this town ever had. Grady had run around with her some before he married Dorothy Eden and maybe some afterwards too. Anyway they got together at the game and renewed old times. They both got drunk after the game and spent the night together in the new motel.

"I reckon it purty near broke Irma's heart, but she taken him back just like it never had happened. But she never could get him back on the wagon for any length of time after that. Nearly every weekend he'd get on a tear; and sometimes the city marshal would have to lock him up to keep him outa trouble. Irma would bale him out and cry over him and doctor him up and get him back on the job Monday mornin'. This went on for months and years.

"But one Monday mornin' when Grady was probably still shaky from his weekend bender, he drove his road grader over a bluff and landed in a creek twenty feet below with the grader on top him. It killed him deader'n a doornail.

"But there was a good side to it. He had $10,000 in life insurance — not that he had ever taken it out himself, but seem like the State of Texas insured all of its highway employees for that amount. Anyway, Irma got the $10,000. She given Grady a nice funeral up at

Frank Porter's new funeral home; and then she taken the rest of the money and started a new cafe.

"At first she was in a rented building over on the north side of the square, but she done so good — she'd always been a good cook and it turned out she was a good businessman too — that she built a new building of her own out at the edge of town on the Fort Worth highway. She's still out there and doin' fine — it's as good a place to eat as you'll find between here and Fort Worth.

"So you see gettin' hisself killed with that road grader was the nicest thing he coulda done for her. That'll be nine-fifty for the gasoline and four dollars for the oil change. It's always good to see an old friend like you. Stop by again when you come this way."

## The Case of the Laughing Hold-Up Victims

If you're not old enough to have lived through the Great Depression of the 1930's, this may not mean much to you. I did live through it—just barely — and maybe I can help you younger people understand how it was in those days.

I graduated from high school in the middle of the 1930's and I wanted to go to college, but my folks were in pretty hard shape just then. We had a big family and my father had had two salary cuts. Under the circumstances, I did the best I could. I accepted an athletic scholarship at Howard Baker College. It was a denominational school with academic standards almost as high as those of a good high school.

In return for playing football, basketball and base-ball— they didn't make me come out for track — I got room and board of a sort and tuition, but not a cent of money. It really wasn't too bad, though. There were enough pretty girls around to make it interesting and we had a fairly good football team. You don't take things too hard when you're young anyway. I enjoyed catching a pass and going for a touchdown regardless of how the economy was doing. And I made some good friends. My roommate, Joe Johnson, was one of the best boys I've ever known. He and I played the same position, left end. If we kicked off, I started; if the other team kicked off, he started. Then the coach would alternate us every quarter or so. One night in the winter after the football season was over and the weather was getting pretty chilly, Joe and I were walking back to the campus from a picture show downtown. Neither of us had an overcoat and a right brisk norther was blowing.

"I've got a dime, ten cents, the tenth part of a dollar left," I said. "Let's go in here at the drug-store and have a cup of coffee."

"That sounds good to me," Joe said, "I'm freezing."

We went into Mac's drug-store. Red Mahoney, the boy who handled the soda fountain and the lunch counter, was the only person there.

"What'll it be?" he said.

"Two cups of java," I said.

He drew them for us, and we sat there sipping the coffee slowly, not a bit anxious to get back out into that cold wind. In a few minutes the front door opened and two funny looking characters sort of sidled in. They both had toboggan caps pulled down to their eyes, and one of them had a pistol.

They eased over toward the soda fountain.

"Stick 'em up," the one with the gun said to Red, "this is a hold-up."

"Think of that," Red said and stuck up his hands, still holding a dish towel in one of them. "Could you let me finish wiping off this counter first?"

"No, get 'em up and keep 'em up."

Then the gunman turned to Joe and me.

"Lay down on the floor over there and keep quiet," he told us.

"Sure," I said, "anything you say, sir."

We laid down on the floor. The linoleum was cold.

"Is there anybody else in here?" the gunman asked Red.

"Gladys," Red said.

"Who's Gladys?"

"She's the colored girl that washes dishes."

"Where is she?"

"Back in the back."

"Get her up here."

"Gladys!" Red yelled.

"What ya want?" Gladys yelled back

"Come up here."

Gladys came. "What ya want now?" she said.

"These gentlemen want to see you," Red said, indicating the bandits.

"What you all want?"

"Lay down on the floor over there," the gunman told her. "You get over there, too," he told Red.

They came over and laid down by Joe and me.

"Where's the money?" the gunman asked.

"In the cash register, of course," Red said, "Where'd you think it would be?"

Both bandits went behind the soda fountain and started fooling with the cash register. Red started laughing. You could tell it wasn't a deliberate laugh — he just couldn't help it.

"What's so funny?" I whispered to him.

"They ain't but thirty cents — three dimes — in that cash register. Mac went home at ten o'clock and took all of the money with him. And I haven't sold but thirty cents worth since then, including your dime."

"That was the last dime I had in the world," I whispered back to him.

"I've got the same amount you have," Joe whispered — "namely not a cryin' dime."

And then all three of us broke out laughing all over the place. We couldn't keep from it.

"What're you-all laughin' about," the gunman asked. "First it's whisperin' and now it's laughin'. I'm gettin' tired of it. This is a *holdup*, I'm tellin' you!"

"Yes, sir," Red said, "excuse us."

"What you-all laughin' about?" Gladys asked.

"Your panties are showing," Red said, "and we think that's funny."

"No, they ain't; I got my skirt pulled down far's it'll go."

"How does this damn cash register work?" the gunman asked.

"Push the *No Sale* button, and it'll open," Red said.

We heard it open.

"Where's the money?" The gunmen asked. "There ain't but thirty cents here."

"Is that a fact?" Red said, "I thought there was over a thousand dollars in there. Maybe you better look again."

The gunman looked carefully, "Three dimes is all there is," he said.

"I bet I know what happened," Red said, "I bet Mac put all that money down under that loose board behind the cigar counter when he left."

"Where's that?" the gunman asked.

"Down behind the cigar counter," Red said. "Feel down there and see if you don't find a loose board in the floor."

The gunman felt around on the floor and got hold of something and pulled.

"It ain't very loose," he complained

"Both of you pull on it," Red said. "It's bound to come up if you pull hard enough."

Both of the bandits got down on the floor behind the cigar counter. Red jumped up and snapped off the light switch by the side of the front door and then raced out the door. It was as dark as a stack of black cats in the drug-store.

"Where's he gone?" the gunman said.

"To get the law," the other bandit said.

"We better get outa here," the gunman said.

"You said it," the other one said.

They scooted out the front door, and we heard them running down the sidewalk.

"Stop that!" Gladys squawked.

"Stop what?" Joe said.

"Stop what you're doin'! I ain't lettin' no white dude prowl my pants, even if they is a hold-up goin' on."

Gladys got up and turned the lights back on. Joe and I got up. Pretty soon Red came back.

"I couldn't find any of the local jawndorms," he said, "but since our brigands are gone, I reckon it don't matter. You gents have another cup of coffee — it's on the house this time."

We sat down at the counter and had another cup of coffee.

"I was kiddin' Gladys about her panties showin'," Red said, "I happen to know she don't have but one pair of panties, and they're in the wash today."

I think Joe could have confirmed this, but he didn't.

# Colonel Cartwright And His Dog, Napoleon

Colonel Ravenel Cartwright was the most aristocratic citizen of Kiowa. He had come to Texas from South Carolina shortly after the close of the Civil War. He had left behind him a cotton sack full of Confederate bonds, a lot of worn-out plantation land and several tumbledown houses, all of which were mortgaged up to their eyebrows. In Texas he tried law, politics, and brandy, of which he liked the brandy the best. Another one of his assets was a very creditable record in the Confederate Army. This he brought with him and exploited to some degree.

When I knew him in the early 1920's he was elderly, widowed, and in declining health. He lived by himself in an old run-down stone house up in the northwest part of town. Dr. Clinton looked in on him every few days and occasionally wrote a new prescription for one of his numerous ailments, and I delivered it. I would knock on the front door and he would yell for me to come in. He was always as courteous as could be. I enjoyed visiting with him and I think he appreciated my visits. He didn't have very much company.

I said he lived by himself. That wasn't quite true; he had a dog. The dog was named Napoleon and he was a remarkable animal. Colonel Cartwright talked to him just as if he were a person. Sometimes, I think, Napoleon thought he *was* a person.

Between the time I opened the front door and the time I reached Colonel Cartwright's bedroom, I could hear him talking to Napoleon.

"Nap," he said, "you're the saddest case I know of. You impress me as being the sawed-off relic of ancient and tragic misfortunes, the ultimate calamity of canine creation, and the offspring of a catastrophic mesalliance."

By the way of reply, Nap snorted.

Sometimes instead of telling Napoleon what a low-down creature he was, the Colonel would read to him. I remember hearing a masterful rendition of Hamlet's soliloquy:

'To be or not to be, that is the question;

Whether 'tis nobler in the mind to suffer the slings and arrows of outrageous fortune," etc.

Napoleon seemed to like it right well, for he snorted twice when the Colonel finished with a magnificent flourish. Snorting appeared to be Napoleon's technique of applause.

And sometimes the Colonel read to him from the Bible, mainly the Psalms and Proverbs. He had a strong, musical voice — he had been lay reader in St. Matthews Episcopal Church since the memory of man runneth not to the contrary — and Napoleon listened raptly to his outpourings.

I tapped on the doorframe and Colonel Cartwright said, "Come in, Cary, if you can tolerate the company of this canine catastrophe for a few minutes."

"I think he's a right fine dog," I said.

"That attitude betrays a commendable Christian charity on your part," the Colonel said.

"I have a new prescription for you," I said.

"Put it there on the table with the others. I may even take some of it. None of Dr. Clinton's stuff does me any good to speak of, but I take it so I won't hurt his feelings."

"He tries hard," I said.

"Yes, I'm sure he does. I'm the party at fault. The sins of my youth are catching up with me. As the scriptures say, 'As ye sow, so shall ye reap', sow the wind and reap the whirlwind; the way of the transgressor is hard; Wine is a mocker and strong drink is raging.'"

"You're being too hard on yourself," I said, "You're

the finest gentleman I know."

"I thank you immensely for that well meant prevarication. Can you stay a few minutes, Cary? There's something I'd like to talk to you about for a while."

"Yes, sir, I can. We aren't very busy at the drug-store these days."

"Thank you, Cary. I'll come to the point. I know I'm not going to last much longer — cirrhosis of the liver and Bright's disease wait for no man — and I'm concerned with what's going to become of Napoleon here when I'm gone. The sorry varmint apparently is going to have the effrontery to out live me — very inconsiderate of him, of course. Nevertheless, I feel some moral obligation to provide for him."

"I'm not surprised," I said.

"Do you know of anybody who might be willing to take Napoleon and look after him in his declining years? I could leave a modest bequest to cover the expenses."

"I'd be glad to do it myself, Colonel," I said, "except that I'm going off to the University of Texas to study law next September. But I think I know who will do it. As you may know, Claude Vance has a big kennel out south of town where he raises bird dogs. I feel confident that he would be willing to take Napoleon and keep him along with the rest of his dogs."

Claude Vance was an old bachelor who lived out south of town. He was supposed to breed bird dogs for sale, and I reckon he did sell one now and then, but mainly he just collected dogs of all sorts and conditions. He did a little farming along with his dog business, and that probably enabled him to survive.

"Claude is a reliable man, I think," I said.

"Yes, I think he is," Colonel Cartwright agreed.

"Well, Cary, you talk to him and see if we can work

out an agreement. As you may have suspected, Napoleon isn't really as calamitous as I sometimes imply and I'll rest easier if some provision is made for him."

"Yes sir, I'll get in touch with Claude right away and I'm sure we can make a good deal with him. He loves dogs."

"I'll appreciate that a great deal," Colonel Cartwright said, and I knew he meant it.

"I better be getting back to the drug-store now,' I said. "If we were to miss a sale by making a customer wait, Mr. Brown would probably die from high blood pressure."

"Thank you very much, Cary," the Colonel said.

I did call Claude Vance and he said he'd be glad to take Napoleon as a boarder when the time came.

"I don't know what the Colonel's idea is about how much he should pay for Napoleon's keep," I said.

"It don't matter," Claude said. "I won't put out any more food to speak of and I have plenty of empty kennels." The time came pretty quickly. Colonel Cartwright died about two weeks after my last visit with him and the Sons of Confederate Veterans gave him a magnificent funeral service. The evening after the funeral I borrowed Mr. Brown's Model T roadster and went up to the Colonel's house and picked up Napoleon. He was a little leery about getting into the car with me, but I finally persuaded him and I took him out to Claude's place and left him.

A week or two later I called Claude and asked him how Napoleon was getting along.

"He ain't doin' a speck o' good, I'm sorry to say," Claude said. "He won't eat and he won't have anything to do with the rest o' the dogs. I'm plumb worried about him."

"That's bad," I said. And then I thought of something.

"Claude," I said, "try reading the Bible or some of Shakespeare to him. And every now and then tell him how lowdown and good for nothing he is."

"*What?*" Claude said.

"I mean it," I said, "The Colonel used to read those kinds of things to him and in between readings he'd tell him what a total loss he was."

"That sounds crazy," Claude said.

"It *is* crazy," I said, "but it might work."

"I'll try it," Claude said, "if I can get a hold of some of them things to read to him."

A few' days later Claude called me and said, "Cary, I want to report the resurrection of Napoleon. Believe it or not, I did what you said and he just laps it up. He eats fine and plays with the other dogs."

"What did you read to him?" I asked.

"I couldn't find no Shakespeare nor Hamlet around my place so I just read him the Bible. I started with the Sermon on the Mount — that's the part of the Bible that I like the best — but he seemed to be a little uneasy with that, so I switched to the Psalms and Isaiah. He liked them much better. I reckon he's an Old Testament dog at heart. However, he still looked a little unsatisfied when I finished reading, so I said, 'You lousy, ungrateful varmint, that's all you're getting this time.' He looked plumb happy after that. Anyway, the whole thing is a miracle. I think I'm gonna start goin' to church."

"That's fine," I said. "You can depend on it that Colonel Cartwright, wherever he is, will bless you for what you have done for Napoleon."

## Upward Mobile

Beauregarde Smith had been the town scavenger. He cleaned out people's closets and for that worthy service he charged an honest dollar and a half a month. With the money he kept, he and his family bought a little frame house across the creek. On this house he paid the taxes and spread a coat of new green paint.

But misfortune had overtaken him. The town government of Kiowa floated a bond issue and put in a new sewer system. This practically ruined the demand for Beauregarde's service. He went out of business, sat on the courthouse lawn with the rest of the loafers, and exhorted them against the evils of socialism.

He came into the drug-store one afternoon to get some of the free ice water that we provided.

"How are you, Mr. Smith? " I asked.

"Cary," he said, "I'm plumb tee-totally rurned. This socialistic new sewer system has put me out of business. I don't know what I'm gonna do. What little money I have saved is gonna be gone purty soon, and after that I don't know what's a comin'."

I felt sorry for him and I told him so.

"It just ain't right," he said. "I'm what Colonel Brandon calls 'private enterprise', and he says private enterprise is what has made this country big and strong. And here this communist city council comes along and stops my business and ruins my life."

I tried to do some thinking while he was drinking the ice water. I thought of something.

"Mr. Smith," I said, "you ought to get into the public utility field."

"What's that? " he asked.

"It's like this," I said, "I read in this week's *Kiowa Chieftain* that the city council is going to start a street-sweeping service here in Kiowa, especially on the courthouse square. You know the farmers come in here and tie their wagons and teams around the square and by the time they go home in the evening the horses and mules have messed up the square mighty bad. Now you've had a lot of experience with that kind of stuff and I'll bet that if you applied for it you could get one of the new jobs. I don't know what they're going to pay, but it might be about as much as you used to make in your old business. You go over and see the mayor this very afternoon and tell him that you're interested in getting one of the jobs. And if he wants you to file a formal application, you get the necessary papers and bring them back here and I'll help you fill them out. You see, I'm going to study law and be a lawyer and I need to start getting some experience in things like this."

"That sounds like a plumb good idee," Beauregarde said. "I shore thank you, Cary." And he lit out for the City Hall.

It turned out that he really did get one of the jobs. He came in to tell me about it.

"Cary, I'm gonna be the boss of the crew. There's gonna be a three-man crew', and I'm gonna be the foreman. That's because of the experience I've done had. And furthermore, I'm gonna get fifty dollars a month while the other two get thirty. And still more furthermore, I can do my work in the daytime like a Christian. In my old business I had to do it all at night."

He was really happy. As he went out the door, he turned and philosophied: "Maybe this socialism ain't so bad after all."

But this wasn't the end of it. When I came back from my second year at the University. I got off the train and walked up Depot Street toward the courthouse square. I was somewhat amazed to see a huge street-sweeping machine coming down the street next to the curb. Up on top of it in the driver's seat sat none other than my old friend and protégé', Beauregarde Smith. He saw me and stopped.

"How ya doin', Cary?" he said. "I'm shore glad to see you."

"Just fine," I said, "and how're you? "

"The best I've ever been," he said, "and as you can see, I've got the best job I've ever had and I owe a lot of it to you. Soon as I heard the City was gonna get this machine, I went down to Howard's garage and started workin' nights and Saturday for nothin' to learn how to drive a contraption like this and take care of it. The mayor offered me the job without me even askin' for it. I'm sure glad you recommended me to get into the public utility business. It looks like I've got a plumb talent for it."

## The Kiowa Papoose Laundry and Fertilizer Mill

Dr. Blaine was another one of the doctors who hung around the drug-store. His office, like Dr. Clinton's, was upstairs over the drug-store. Neither of the doctors had a nurse or a receptionist or anything like that, so they put a phone in the drug-store and expected Bill and me to answer it for them. We put a Prince Albert tobacco can down over the bell of the phone so it would have a different sound from that of the drug-store phone. In return for this telephone service and a lot of other things we did for them, the doctors brought all their prescriptions for us to fill.

Dr. Blaine practiced medicine after a fashion, but mostly he was an inventor. Or, I should say, he worked on inventions. Most of them he never finished, but he liked to talk to Bill and me about them. When the racketeers in Chicago were breaking out the show windows of all who refused to pay for "protection," he started working on a break-proof glass. It appeared to him that it could be possible to develop a kind of glass that would bend but not break. Then it could be straightened up again after the attack was over. He never quite got the details worked out, but he talked about it for a long time.

He worked on a hydraulic peanut crusher for a long time also and finally came up with a working model of a sort, but he couldn't persuade the International Harvester Company to manufacture it on a commercial scale.

He got into the field of political economy and high finance too. He noticed that some of the paper money which was in circulation at the time consisted of what amounted to warehouse receipts for either silver or gold and that other kinds were simply unsecured promises of the government to pay at no specified time. His strategy was simplicity itself. When he got hold of one of the silver or gold certificates, he would hang on to it, thus confining his expenditures to the unsecured promises to pay. He pursued this attack for some time but since his total income was severely limited, he found that he had to use any and all kinds of money that he could get a hold of to cover his expenses. I don't think the United States Treasury ever felt any effect of his program.

But the project that was dearest to the heart of Dr. Blaine was the development of a machine that would do two things: First it would launder badly soiled baby's diapers, and second, it would convert the residue into fertilizer. (This, of course, was before the time of disposable paper diapers.)

He exhorted Bill and me on the merits of the project.

"There's no household chore that women (not to mention men) hate more than washing badly soiled diapers. It's a filthy, demeaning task. Any mother would give a great deal to be relieved of it and if their husbands have to do it, they would pay even more to be rid of it."

"Now what I propose to do is to launder the diapers free of charge. That would assure us of an abundant and unending supply of raw material for the other end of the operation. That is the use of the residue from the laundering to make a highly potent fertilizer for farm crops. Human excretion has been extensively used as a fertilizer. The Chinese have used it for centuries. They call it night soil. It's all that has enabled them to feed their teeming millions on the very limited area of available land which they have. But it isn't necessary to go to far-away China to find a place that needs it. This sandy land right here in Kiowa County on which the farmers grow peanuts has a crying need of a good nitrogenous fertilizer. We'll mix the residue with sand, and the good Lord knows that we have plenty of sand in this area. That takes care of the physical production of our life-giving product. All that remains to be done is to market the output, and that should be the easiest part of all. As soon as the farmers learn about our product, they'll buy every grain of it that we can produce.

He paused to light his pipe, which had gone out.

"Who is 'we' in this scheme?" Bill asked.

"Why you and Cary and myself for the time being," Dr. Blaine said. "Later on we may offer stock for sale to the general public."

"I don't have any money to put into anything," Bill said. Bill spent all of his money on girls, mostly before he even got it. He had charge accounts all over town. He was a good boy, but girls were his weakness.

"I know you don't have any money," Dr. Blaine said. "We'll put you in charge of the Sales Department on a commission basis."

Bill looked dubious.

"Cary, you have some money saved up, don't you?" Dr. Blaine asked.

"Yes," I said. "I have a few hundred dollars, but it's going to stay saved up. I'm going to use it to go to college."

"I have a little of my own," Dr. Blaine said, "and I reckon I can borrow a little more at the bank. Cary, we'll put you in charge of the Production Department and I'll supervise the whole operation."

"What do we have to operate? " I asked.

"Sid Elkins down at his tin shop is working on the washing machine part, and he says it will be ready in a week or two. And I have made a most fortunate arrangement for an engine and water heater. We're going to need a lot of hot water, you know. You may remember seeing that old steam tractor sitting in front of Ned Oswell's barn out south of town. He has no further use for it since he bought a new gasoline model, and has offered to sell it to me for five dollars provided I take off his premises. Shelley Gray knows how to run it, and I have hired him to bring it in and station it back of the drug store here."

"Does Mr. Brown know about this? " I asked.

"Yes, and he's all for it. He sees that the delivery and pick-up of the diapers will bring a lot of potential customers into the drug-store. When the women come in, they'll see things and want to buy them. It's simply amazing how many things there are that women rather have than money."

"I've noticed that." I said.

"I've made a deal with Gabe Hopson to bring in several wagon loads of sand so we're practically ready to start."

"What are we going to use for fuel to stoke that old steam engine? " I asked.

"The oil mill people have agreed to sell me a couple of tons of coal. They have a lot on hand and won't need it till they start running next fall," the doctor said.

I could see that he was taking this thing seriously. He went on talking.

"We need a name, of course, and we'll have to do a little advertising at first to let the public know what we're doing."

"I can think of a good name." Bill said.

"What's that? " Dr. Blaine said.

"I think we ought to call it the Kiowa Papoose Laundry and Fertilizer Company." Bill said, "and our trade mark should be a picture of our Indian baby with peanut vines growing all around him. And then under the picture in big letters we ought to say KIOWA PAPOOSE FERTILIZER—IT'S SO STRONG IT'S A

BARGAIN AT ANY PRICE!"

"That sounds good," Dr. Blaine said, and I agreed.

It took us about two weeks to get everything lined up and ready to go. As soon as people realized that we would launder diapers for free, the diapers came pouring in. That part of the enterprise was a huge success, at least at the start. Sid Elkins had cooked up a right good washing machine. It had a big dasher to bat the diapers around and a filter across the bottom to catch the residue and roll it out into a big tub. The old steam tractor, once it was lubricated and cleaned up, ran surprisingly well. It turned the washing machine and provided hot water from the boiler. The first run came out just as the doctor had ordered. I was right proud of the Production Department of the Kiowa Papoose Laundry and Fertilizer Company.

But from the very start we had trouble with the Sales Department. Bill was undoubtedly a good salesman when he was working with cosmetics and patent medicine, but he didn't know beans about peanut farming or anything of the kind. And the season was against him. It was the first week of June when we got started, and that was too late to do any fertilizing of that year's crops. And also the farmers didn't have any money to speak of at that time of the year. They wouldn't have any until they had harvested and sold their crops in the fall.

And then we soon found out that there was some opposition from the women too. Somehow they didn't like to have their babies associated in any way with Kiowa Papooses and peanut fertilizers. Maybe this feeling wasn't rational but it was potent just the same.

And also our advertising budget was very limited. Dr. Blaine had spent all the money he could raise on the Production Department, so he had to get the advertising on credit. And he didn't have the best credit rating in Kiowa for the very simple reason that he had a way of not paying his bills on time, if at all.

Altogether we just didn't sell enough of our output to amount to a hill of beans.

But as I said before, one part of the business flourished. The diapers kept pouring in. Women all over Kiowa County sent their diapers to us and furthermore they told their kinfolks and friends in surrounding counties about our free service. Pretty soon a truck-load was coming in from Post Oak City twice a week and we couldn't keep up with the traffic. We had been storing the newly arrived diapers in the back room of the drug-store, but after a day or two of hot weather they smelled awful. They were stinking up the whole drug-store. Mr. Brown said that would have to stop. I didn't blame him for putting his foot down.

I found an old empty shed out back of the drug-store where Martin's used to store farm implements, and I worked half the night moving our surplus of raw material out there. This eased our problems for the moment, but it didn't last. The neighbors who lived in the block just north of the old shed began to complain about the odor. I couldn't blame them either, of course.

By this time it was the last of June, and everybody was getting ready for the Fourth of July celebration. There was to be a big parade around the courthouse square in the morning, a watermelon feast in the afternoon, a big fireworks display at night. Not too much ever happened in Kiowa so everybody was looking forward to the celebration.

Maybe you think that the drug-store would be closed on the Fourth of July, but if you do, it shows that you don't know Mr. London Brown. In the first year I worked for him, I worked 364 days out of 365. I got Christmas day off. He didn't take even that much off. He came down Christmas afternoon and opened the store.

He couldn't help it. He was just that way. His drug-store was the biggest thing in his life.

So on the Fourth of July I jerked soda all day long and into the night. I kept the big washing machine going too, because it wouldn't do for us to get any further behind than we already were.

Just before eight o'clock when the fireworks were scheduled to start out on the courthouse square, I went back and shoveled in a lot of coal — enough that I wouldn't have to look after it during the celebration. Maybe I overdid it a bit. And since there weren't any customers in the drug-store at the time, I went out in front and sat down on the curb to watch the first roman candles go up. A little breeze had come up so it was almost comfortable out there, and I relaxed and enjoyed the show.

The fireworks lasted about an hour. When the courthouse clock struck nine, Buck Masters, who was in charge, announced that the display would end with "a giant rocket — the biggest and best that Kiowa has ever seen. Hold your breath folks till it goes off. It's going to be awesome!" It took a minute or two for them to set the big rocket in its socket and light the fuse. Then it arched into the night sky showering sparks in all directions. It was an exciting sight.

And then came the biggest bang I had ever heard in my life. It fairly rocked the front of the drug-store, and sticks and bricks began to rain down, and people were screaming and yelling everywhere.

"That," I said to myself, "is overdoing it. They ought not to use rockets as big as that."

But the rocket wasn't all that had exploded. I looked in at front door of the drug-store and I could see all the way through the back. There was a hole in the back wall that you could have driven a hay wagon through, and a fire was burning briskly around the place where the Kiowa Papoose Laundry and Fertilizer Company's Production Department had been. Gradually I figured it out. The boiler had exploded just as the rocket went off.

Everybody who had been watching the fireworks display now came running over to the drug-store to see what had happened. It was worse than a riot. Since the wreckage was out back, the crowd had to run through the front of the drug-store. They wrecked that part just about as badly as the boiler had wrecked the rear.

I got to the telephone and called the Fire Department, but nobody answered. Bob Holland, the chief of the Kiowa Volunteer Fire Department, had evidently gone to the celebration. But he must have seen or heard about the fire in some other way because in just a few minutes the fire truck came swinging around the First National Bank corner with about half the crowd hanging on to it. They got the fire put out pretty quickly. It wasn't a very big fire, mainly because there wasn't anything left around there to be burned.

After the fire was out, the crowd quieted down a little, and it looked like the extravaganza might be over. But then another unfortunate event took place. The bulk of the people had drifted back out to the front of the drug-store, and just then a big truck drove up. I gasped. It was the truck from Post Oak City bringing the semi-weekly load of raw material for our one-time laundry.

I went out and spoke to the driver.

"You better just turn around and take that stuff back to Post Oak City. The Kiowa Papoose Laundry and Fertilizer Company has just gone out business — I mean *way* out."

The crowd gathered around the truck and the driver. There were two things wrong with the driver: (1) He was black, and (2) He had unwelcome cargo on board. The crowd was in a high state of excitement.

They were disappointed that the fire had been put out so quickly. They felt they had been cheated.

I should say at this point that there weren't any Negroes in Kiowa County. They had all been chased out by a mob back in the 1880's. So that was another thing wrong with the truck driver. I could tell that something was cooking in the crowd.

"You better get out of here in a hurry," I told him, "This crowd isn't too friendly."

He saw my point. He shoved the truck into gear and went tearing off in the direction of Post Oak City. Somehow that riled the crowd even worse. They didn't want him in Kiowa, but they didn't want him to escape just punishment for coming. Men began to run to their cars and start in pursuit of the foully-loaded truck and its driver.

But the driver had a pretty good start on them, so they didn't catch him before he got out of town. Even Randy Bradford in his Stutz Bearcat had to drive about five miles out on the Post Oak City road before he found the truck pulled off on the shoulder. The driver had evidently took off across the big Bryson pasture. We never did see him again.

One of the boys with Randy wanted to bring the truck back to Kiowa and drive it around the courthouse to show the people that they had captured it, but the driver had taken the keys with him so they couldn't start the truck. It stayed there for a long time — several weeks, in fact — till the owner finally came over from Post Oak City and towed it back there.

I reckon that was the last episode in the short life of the Kiowa Papoose Laundry and Fertilizer Company.

P.S. Mr. Smith and the local agent managed to stretch his insurance policy to cover all of the damage to the drug-store. In fact, he made a considerable profit on the deal. This pleased him so much that he almost forgave Bill and me for our part in the catastrophe.

P.S. No. 2. Dr. Blaine started working on a reciprocating lightning rod that would start a sprinkler system in case a house was struck by lightning.

P.S. No. 3. People all said it was the most exciting Fourth of July Kiowa had ever had.

# The Kiowa Chieftain Contest

The *Kiowa Chieftain* was the weekly newspaper published in Kiowa. Its office and printing plant were right next door to the drug-store. Every two or three years the owner-publisher-editor-printer, Mr. Cicero Jester, would stage a big contest. Anybody who wanted to could enter it. The idea was for the contestants to sell subscriptions to the *Chieftain*. The price of a subscription was $1.50 for one year or $2.00 for two years or $3.00 for five years. For the first prize there was an Overland sedan, the second prize was an electric refrigerator, and the third prize was a one-year scholarship to Howard Baker College, a jerk-water denominational school over in Post Oak City. There were several smaller prizes that I don't remember— maybe a set of dishes or a toaster or something like that. The contest was to last three months: June, July and August.

There must have been fifteen or twenty people who entered the contest at first. Among them was Mrs. Amy Lou Comstock. Mrs. Comstock was a widow about sixty years old. Her husband had died from tuberculosis several years before and she had made a living of a sort after his death by giving piano lessons. She had lots of friends in Kiowa, and she was leading the pack when the first standings were published in the *Chieftain*. This encouraged her greatly and she redoubled her efforts, as Colonel Brandon would say. In the heat and drought of July she walked all over the town of Kiowa soliciting subscriptions. Nearly everybody who could read was already a subscriber, so it was hard for her to get new subscribers. So in the even worse heat and drought of August, she began to walk out the country roads and solicit the farm people.

She was thin and wispy to begin with, and two

months of the sort of exercise she was getting made her downright spectre-like. She stopped at the drug-store one evening after working the sandy land out north of town to get some of our free ice water, and I judged she didn't weigh more than eighty or eighty-five pounds. And she was as brown as a Mexican. I felt sorry for her, "Mrs. Comstock," I said, "you oughtn't to get out into this hot sun and dust and walk all day like you're doing. It'll kill you."

"No, it won't, Cary," she said, "I'm tough and I've simply got to win that car. I need it so badly to meet my piano classes."

"But those sandy-land farmers aren't going to subscribe for a newspaper. A lot of them can't read anything beyond RJR on a sack of smoking tobacco; and also they don't have any money."

"A few of them do, and I simply must stay ahead in the race."

She drank another glass of ice water and started walking home.

But if she had a hard time getting new subscribers, so did the other contestants, and she continued to hold the top spot. So by the beginning of the last week of August, it looked like she would surely get the top prize, the new sedan. Nearly everybody was rooting for her. She was definitely the peoples' choice.

Then two days before the contest was to end, Dr. Gage, who was going to buy a new car anyway, subscribed for the *Chieftain* for a hundred years for himself and another hundred for each of his two children. He had been running way down in the pack, but this outburst put him so far ahead of everybody that there was no chance of overtaking him in the two days left.

Furthermore, it turned out that Lula Greenspan, who had been running second to Mrs. Comstock, had been holding out on her weekly reports. On the very last day she turned in 135 subscriptions that she hadn't reported before. She got the electric refrigerator.

That put Mrs. Comstock in third place, so she got the scholarship to Howard Baker College. When she read the fine print she discovered that it covered only the entrance fee, and it was non-transferable. Since she already had a bachelor's degree from Ward Belmont, she had about as much use for a year at Howard Baker as a hog has for a sidesaddle.

I pretty nearly lost my religion over that case.

# The Church Attendance Contest

Mrs. Courtney Pendergrass had switched from the Baptist Church to the Methodist Church and back again three times in the years that I could remember. I don't think the changes had anything to do with doctrine or theology or anything like that. It was simply that Mrs. Pendergrass wanted to run whatever church she was in at the time. If the rest of the members kept her from running things to her own liking, she changed churches. The people in the church she left didn't seem to mourn her departure except for one thing: Her husband, Mr. John Pendergrass, was one of the three richest men in Kiowa County and although he wasn't much of a church-goer himself, he let his wife make handsome contributions to the church she was currently favoring with her membership. So when she pulled out of one of the churches, she left something of a budgetary crisis behind her. That, of course, was bad for the abandoned denomination.

Mrs. Courtney Pendergrass's mother-in-law, Old Lady Moses Pendergrass, was a dyed-in-the-wool Baptist, and she wouldn't have switched to the Methodists or any other denomination if the Holy Ghost Himself had come down and told her to. She was about ninety years old and looked a lot like Mrs. Devil. She looked upon her daughter-in-law's flighty transfers as nothing short of cardinal sin. She and her husband, Old Moses, had come to Kiowa County back in the 1870's. Moses' first job was digging post-holes on the Stone ranch for 75 cents a day and board. His wife cooked for twelve cowhands on an open fireplace for her board. Over the years they had come to own the biggest ranch in the county.

When Old Moses died some time in the early 1900's, he left everything to his wife. She had proclaimed publicly that she would see her daughter-in-law in nethermost hell before she would allow that party to get one cent of her money.

I trust you get the picture.

In the late summer of 1921 the Kiowa County Ministerial Association, which in theory if not in fact, included every minister of the gospel in Kiowa County regardless of his denominational connections, cooked up a big contest in which every church was to participate. The idea was to promote church attendance and general participation in church affairs. During the three months of September, October, and November, every church was to keep strict account of the number of people attending any and all of its meetings— regular church services, prayer meetings, young peoples' meetings, Sunday school classes, weddings, funerals, conventions, and what not.

Everybody knew in advance that either the Baptists or the Methodists would win. None of the other denominations could even approach them in numbers, but still the smaller denominations, like the Presbyterians and the Campbellites, thought they might beat some other small denomination. The Episcopalians knew they couldn't beat anybody, but since they were sort of proud of their reputation for being small and exclusive, they were willing to enter the contest and show just how small and selective they were.

Each church sent in weekly reports to the Association, and these were totaled and published in the *Chieftain*. All through the first two and a half months of the contest, the lead seesawed between the First Baptist Church and the First Methodist in the town of Kiowa. Neither one of them could ever come up with a commanding lead. This was somewhat frustrating for both camps, but it also stimulated them to greater and greater effort. New activities — cooking schools, Boy Scouts, Girl Scouts, sewing clubs, Bible study, and any number of others — were organized. In a way it was another Great Awakening.

About the middle of November, Old Lady Moses Pendergrass went into sort of a decline. She went to bed, quit eating, and refused to take the medicines that Dr. Gage prescribed for her. She was close to ninety-one years old and it looked like the end. She sent for Colonel Brandon, her lawyer, and had him make a few changes in her final will and testament. She also called for the pastor of the First Baptist Church to come up to her house and extend the Lord's forgiveness for some minor sins that she had overlooked before.

The situation sent her daughter-in-law into shock. Mrs. Courtney had just gone through a particularly stormy withdrawal from the Baptist bastion and she was hell-bent on defeating them in the big contest, thereby punishing them justly for their insubordination. Now with her mother-in law's close approach to death, she panicked.

She came into the drug-store and outlined her problem to me.

"Cary," she said, "you've just got to help me. I can't get Dr. Gage to do anything beyond what he has already done, and none of the other doctors will do anything at all as long as he is on her case. As you probably know, the Old Lady and Old Man are kin to half of the people in Kiowa County, and most of the other half owe them money. So if she dies now, it'll be the biggest funeral this county has ever seen. Everybody and his dog will come to it, and the Baptists will win the contest. Cary, you've just got to help me. If you can find some kind of medicine here in the drug-store that will keep that old hellcat alive till after the first day of December, I'll pay you five hundred dollars cash money."

"Mrs. Pendergrass," I said, "I couldn't take money for anything like that because I'm not a licensed physician, but I do know of something we have here that might help your mother-in-law in her declining days. I suspect that her problem is at least partly psychological and I think that the new drug I have in mind may do a great deal to lift her spirits. I'll be glad to sell you three bottles of it at the regular price of $1.50 a bottle, and I'll deliver it and advise the patient about the dosage."

"Take the old bitch six bottles of it if you think it would do her any more good," Mrs. Courtney said, "and charge it to my account."

What I was thinking about, of course, was Dr. Helium's Spring Tonic and System Purifier which, as I have mentioned before, was about sixty-percent grain alcohol. After Mrs. Courtney left I wrapped up three bottles of the wonder worker and took them up to the elder Pendergrass's mansion. I had some pretty sound evidence that the patient would respond to the treatment I was offering. All of us at the drug-store knew that she loved a drink a little better than her own right eye. Prohibition had been a bitter blow for the Pendergrass family.

I knocked at the front door and somebody yelled for me to come in. I found the Old Lady in her upstairs bedroom. "Hello, Cary," she said, "what've you got there? "

"It's an old remedy with a new name," I said. "I think you'll like it. Also it may restore your zest for life in addition to relieving your physical symptoms."

"It would take four full quarts of Old Granddad to do that," she said.

"This preparation has something in common with Old Granddad," I said. "Let me fix a dose of it for you."

I took a glass off her bedside table and poured about

four ounces of Dr. Helium's elixir into it and filled it up with ice water from the pitcher.

"You sip this slowly," I said, "and I think you'll feel a lot better very shortly."

She sniffed the glass.

"Cary, I think you have the remedy for my condition."

"Repeat the dose about every hour, and let me know when the prescription needs refilling," I said.

"I'll do that," she said.

I am happy to report that the elder Mrs. Pendergrass lived six more years, to the ripe old age of ninety-seven, so the Baptists were deprived of the opportunity to stage a super-funeral during the contest.

"Cary," she told me, "I've enjoyed the treatment you've given me, but I never had any intention of dying during that contest. I just wanted to scare the whey out of ol' Courtney."

P.S. The Baptists won the contest anyway. You just couldn't out do the Baptists in Kiowa County, Texas, in those days. I think that is probably still true and also all over Texas. Baylor even wins a Southwest Conference championship in football every fifty years or so.

## "It Just Don't Pay To Be Too Close To The Preacher"

Bill and I were leaning on the cigar case during a lull in business. We were always so tired that we leaned on something whenever we weren't busy waiting on customers. This was during the oil boom and the influenza epidemic, you understand.

Mrs. Tutwiler came in. She was the wife of Levi Tutwiler, the traveling preacher, the mother of Mattie May Tutwiler, and so the mother-in-law of Ham McCurdy, all of whom you have heard about before. She was as pregnant as a Percheron mare. She already had eleven children and was clearly headed for a round dozen.

She walked up as close to the soda fountain as she could get under the circumstances and ordered a Coca-Cola. I made it for her. She picked it up and walked around behind the candy case, which was a little taller than she was. We wondered why she did this, and she told us.

"I don't want my husband to see me in here. He thinks it's a sin to drink a coke. Maybe it is — he knows more about sin than anybody else in the world, I reckon — but I have a cravin' for a coke when I'm like I am now. And I'm this way just about all the time."

"Does your husband drink coffee," Bill asked.

"Yes, he drinks a cup of coffee every chance he gets — six or eight cups a day, I'd reckon."

"Tell him there's more caffeine in a cup of coffee than there is in glass of Coca-Cola."

"I'll tell him but it won't do any good. He thinks anything he does is the will o' God and has to be right."

"Sounds like a preacher," Bill said.

"You don't know the half of it. He's that way about havin' children, too. Says children come from God. Says the Bible says to be fruitful and multiply over all the earth. But it's me that has to do the multiplying and I've just about multiplied out."

"We could sell you something that would stop that." Bill was always the salesman.

"I know they are such things, but I wouldn't feel right about usin' 'em. He says that usin' anything like that is agin nature and God and is pure sin."

"He wouldn't have to know about it. We can fix you up with a device that you can insert yourself, and he'd never know about it."

"He'd find out some way, and then there'd be all hell to pay."

"I believe you're just afraid of him."

"There's no question about that. You would be, too, if you was in my place."

She paid me a nickel for the coke and started to leave. At the door she turned and gave us sort of a summation:

"It just don't pay to be too close to the preacher."

# The Ewing-Bradford Feud

People have wondered about the Ewing-Bradford feud. An understanding of it takes some explaining.

The Ewing family was a big one with a long pedigree. They claimed to have come to Texas with Stephen F. Austin's Old Three Hundred, and they probably had. They had lots of old papers and records that were said to prove it. They never seemed to have much money, but they had what Colonel Brandon called "standing" in the town.

John Ewing was next to the oldest of the Ewing boys. He had grown up in Kiowa, but he had gone away to school at the University of Texas and then to Harvard for a graduated degree. After that he had taught in several universities around over the country and worked for the Government in Washington during the New Deal era. Also, he had written several books and was beginning to be considered something of a Great Man.

In his early middle age he came back to Kiowa and bought the old Holman Place. This old house had once been the showplace of Kiowa, but it was badly run down. He undertook to restore it while he continued with more or less serious writing.

Randy Bradford had stuck close to home, but with his father's success in the mercantile business to support him, he was an outstanding local figure; a bachelor and the answer to many a maiden's passionate prayers. He had been a pretty good football player in his younger days and he still had something of the look of a good ball carrier.

One morning shortly after he had moved into the old Holman Place, John Ewing was out in the front yard reworking a neglected flowerbed. Randy Bradford drove up in his Stutz Bearcat — yellow wheels, seven spotlights, acres of chrome, muffler cut out wide open, and the tires slinging gravel. He slowed down at the sight of John in the flowerbed.

Now John could have moved and said "Some boat you've got there."

Or he could have smiled and said, "Where'd you get that rattle-trap?"

Or he could have pretended to be scared by the apparition and run behind the shrubbery.

Or he could have asked, "How many more payments before its yours?"

Any or all of these responses would have been well within the Kiowa tradition, and Randy would have accepted them happily and classified John as a staunch friend and welcomed him back to the old town. The situation was John's ample opportunity to be returned to good standing in the community. But John didn't make any of the appropriate responses. He didn't so much as glance up from his work in the flowerbed. He simply ignored Randy's very existence, not to mention that of the rather obvious Stutz Bearcat.

Randy never forgave him. That was the beginning of the feud.

Randy began to strike back. He had a number of means at his disposal: First of all, he passed the word around that John Ewing (and thus by implication all of the Ewing clan) was stuck-up and considered himself better than the other people in Kiowa. It was an article of passionate faith in Kiowa that one man was as good as another and probably a damn-sight better.

Furthermore, Randy let it be known that John occasionally wrote poetry. Short stories suitable for the *Saturday Evening Post* had their defenders in Kiowa, but poetry, especially poetry that didn't rhyme, had none. (The jewels turned out by Edgar A. Guest were a partial exception to the general rule.)

And then Randy pointed out that John *walked*. In spite of having a perfectly good Oldsmobile in his port cochere, John regularly engaged in the incomprehensible behavior of walking down to the post office every morning to get his mail. And what was even worse, on most evenings he took long walks by himself, not going anywhere in particular. The people distrusted this last quirk badly indeed.

No redneck or ex-redneck who has walked unnumbered miles up and down cotton rows, plowing, chopping, picking, for years on end, can ever understand walking for exercise, relaxation, pleasure, or any related foolishness. When Joe Churchman, a respected citizen of Kiowa, was directed by his doctor to walk ten blocks a day to help him recuperate from a heart attack, Joe was careful to explain to his neighbors that he was doing the walking under his doctor's orders. Some people were dubious about the matter even then. They considered a rest-cure much more appropriate.

So when John Ewing's name came up for admission to the Kiowa Golf and Country Club, Randy had no trouble in getting him black-balled thoroughly. *That* would teach him a lesson, Randy figured.

But this didn't end the matter. Another chapter was in the making. It was in connection with the Centennial of the creation of Kiowa County in 1854. The town of Kiowa and all of Kiowa County were, of course, to participate in the celebration in a big way.

Randy Bradford as the reigning scion of the wealthiest and one of the oldest families in the county assumed a position of leadership in the preparations from the very outset. He appointed committees and called meetings and made arrangements, but none of the Clan Ewing had any part in any of his plans. This, of course, was to be expected under the circumstances.

According to the Master Plan as worked out by Randy's Executive Committee, the first big segment of the Centennial Celebration was to be an Historical Pageant of Kiowa County and as the very first number Randy was to read a short history of the early settlements in the county to "an audience of thousands." Randy was pleased to do the reading of the history — he could read pretty well even when there were a lot of big words — but the writing of it was turned over to a committee, made up mainly of elderly ladies. This committee, in turn, sought help from John Ewing who was clearly the best writer in the county. John prepared a text which pleased the ladies highly, since all of their ancestors were dealt with generously rather than too truthfully,

But on the evening of the presentation, John asked Miss Prunella Pettigrew, President of the Stephen F. Austin-Sam Houston Literary and Drama Society and Chair-Lady of the Committee, for the approved copy, ostensibly to make a last minute correction of a date. Undoubtedly he switched copies and handed Miss Prunella a dastardly doctored document, which she in turn, handed to Randy.

Randy was given a flowery introduction by Miss Prunella and began to read. He intoned that the first permanent white settlement in Kiowa County was made by a group of migrants from Wisconsin, the next state to the north, in the early years of the sixteenth century. Randy saw nothing wrong with this whatsoever. He next informed the audience that these settlers were lead by James Fenimore Cooper, a cotton planter from Illinois. Miss Prunella and the other members of the committee were now in a state of shock too deep to permit their doing anything to halt Randy.

The bloodshed continued: "Twenty-seven of these original settlers were killed in the Battle of the Alamo and thirty-eight others in the Goliad Massacre before their arrival in Kiowa County." Even to Randy some of this statements seemed somewhat improbable. It was not that he had anything against the Alamo or Goliad. Far from it, he held both of them in the highest esteem, but he didn't know too much about them. If someone had asked him when the Fall of the Alamo happened, he would have said, "A long time ago," but whether this meant the sixteenth century or the nineteenth did not concern him. He didn't think such things were worth knowing, and he despised the knowers of such. But for the early settlers to be deceased before their arrival in Kiowa County was a bit much.

"That ain't right, is it?" he said to Miss Prunella in a stage whisper. Unfortunately the stage whisper went squarely into the mike and was transmitted to the "audience of thousands" in fully audible volume. Some of the audience looked blank, some tittered, and some guffawed. All members of the Clan Ewing sat in prim silence.

Miss Prunella revived momentarily and seized the manuscript from the hands of the understandably confused reader.

"You're reading the wrong script!" she hissed at Randy.

"Where's the right one? " he asked in righteous ignorance.

"I don't know," Miss Prunella further hissed, "but for Christs' sake stop reading this one! All of this went into the microphone and thence to the crowd.

To put it mildly, pandemonium reigned and Randy Bradford fell far short of being the hero of the occasion. He looked at the audience. He looked at Miss Prunella. He sat down and lighted a cigarette. He looked a lot like a scared little boy.

I think John Ewing really felt sorry for him at *that* point.

Randy was down but he was not out; he had lost a battle but he hadn't lost the war. In the days ahead he thought of something and sprang into action.

Back of the old Holman Place there was a big vacant lot, two or three acres. Such vacant lots were common all over the town of Kiowa. Randy went to the courthouse and looked this one up. It belonged to the heirs of a couple who had moved out to Lubbock many years before. He got in touch with them and managed to buy the lot for fifty dollars and back taxes. What did he want with it? It was like this:

For years the Bradford Mercantile Company had had a sideline of buying hogs from the farmers in the fall. The small cotton and peanut farmers out north and east of town would each have a few head of hogs to sell but not enough to make a car-load shipment to the packing houses in Fort Worth. Bradford's would buy them at sub-market prices, feed them for a while to bring them up to optimum market weight, and then ship them to Fort Worth. The feeding had been done in a lot down near the railroad tracks.

Randy's plan was simple. He moved the hog operation from the railroad tracks to the lot behind John Ewing's newly restored mansion. He had a hog proof woven-wire fence built around the lot, put in a few sheds for storing feed, and dammed up the only drainage ditch. Then he brought up about two hundred head of hogs from the railroad location.

It turned out to be a rainy fall. In a few weeks the new lot was knee deep in black mud all over and since hogs don't have much notion of sanitation the odor rose to the high heavens and spread over the neighborhood. But John Ewing's household got more of it than anybody else did. Nevertheless, John refrained from making any complaint.

The celebration of Halloween in Kiowa had always been a little on the rowdy side, but this particular one reached new proportions. While some of the youngsters were busy moving outhouses onto the sidewalk in front of the high school and some others were soaping windows and windshields, somebody, quite possibly John Ewing, slipped down into the Bradford hog lot and snipped out two sections of the woven-wire fence. Then whoever it was seemed to have turned a pack of stray dogs into the lot and sicced them on to the hogs. The hogs ran around the lot till they came to the gap in the fence, and then they went through it.

From that point they scattered pretty well all over town. The dogs did a good job of chasing them and they got a lot of help from gangs of teenage boys. They knocked garbage cans over and looted them. They rooted up fall gardens and fouled front porches.

The Ladies' Aid Society of the First Baptist Church had staged a commendable project for keeping small children off the streets by giving a big party for them in the Parish Hall of the church. There were games and refreshments for the guests. Several children came, largely under parental duress, but they didn't stay very long. They wanted to get out where the action was. A good deal of the sandwiches and fruit salad was left.

Mrs. Stanley Brookfield and her helpers were cleaning up and putting things away when the first of the hogs arrived on the scene. The front door of the Hall was open and a big sow stuck her snout inside and sniffed a friendly sniff. Probably she smelled the pimento-cheese sandwich filling and liked it. At any rate she came in, all 340 pounds of her, and ambled amiably back toward the kitchen. Mrs. Brookfield saw her and shrieked. The other ladies shrieked in full support. Mrs. Brookfield grabbed a broom and bravely advanced upon the intruder. The sow was startled by the attack. People who interfere with large animals are apt to get run over, but in this case Mrs. Brookfield got run under. In her wild dash for the front door the sow ran between Mrs. Brookfield's knees. The lady lost her footing and sat down with a thud on the sow's broad back. Somehow the hog's front feet got caught in Mrs. Brookfield's costume and the poor lady was unable to dismount and thus was carried away, still waving the broom and screaming at the top of her lungs.

It was by far the best Halloween act the town of Kiowa had ever seen.

Once out the front door, the hog headed down Houston Street toward the Courthouse Square, but meeting a bunch of hooting boys at the corner by the Ford Station, she made a sharp turn to the right, and Mrs. Brookfield slid off into a ditch that had a lot of rainwater backed up in it. She was quickly rescued by some of the boys and didn't seem to have suffered any bodily harm, but her life was never quite the same again.

Mrs. Brookfield's husband wanted to sue the Bradfords for $50,000, which he figured was about all of the money in the world at that time, but Mrs. Brookfield in her modesty refused to testify in open court. However, she got some consolation out of the fact that it was a female hog rather than a male which had violated her intimate space.

The damage which the Bradford Mercantile Company did have to pay for ran up to something over seven hundred dollars, and that was a lot of money in that time and place. Uncle Rufe Bradford, Randy's father, put his foot down and made Randy move the hog operation back down to the railroad tracks.

At this point the score in the Ewing-Bradford feud was probably about even and it should have stopped there, but it didn't. In the hands of the third and fourth generations of Ewings and Bradfords, it is still alive and well.

# The Saga of Dougal McFrey

Dougal McFrey was one of the boys I grew up with in Kiowa. His father, old Spottswood McFrey, was one of the more successful cotton-buyers in the town back in the days when Kiowa County was an important cotton growing area. Dougal was the oldest of several children in the family. He graduated in the same class from Kiowa High School that I was in and since his father had just had one of his best years in the cotton business, he was willing to send Dougal to the University of Texas.

I'll have to tell you something about Dougal's scholarship. He was very poor in English and he never did get through the first year of Spanish, but he was a shark in math and accounting and anything that had any connection with business or money appealed to him. There were four of us from Kiowa who all lived in the same house at the University and we all had to help Dougal with his English, especially with any writing he had to do.

I had written a review of Thomas Hardy's novel *The Return of the Native* and gotten an *A* on it. Dougal had been given the assignment of writing a paper on the "The Literary Forgeries of Chatterton and McPherson." He figured that an *A* on one topic ought to be good for an *A* on another topic despite the fact that it would be hard to find two topics more unalike than these two. Anyway, he copied about half of what I had written about *The Return of the Native* into his appraisal of the literary shenanigans of Chatterton and McPherson. When he got his paper back it had a flat *F* on it.

He showed it to me in disgust: "This proves that these profs here don't know what they want."

I tried to explain to him that the subject matter in the two cases was considerably different, but I didn't get anywhere with it. He never had any confidence in English teachers.

In addition to being good at math and accounting, Dougal was a lethal chess player. He beat all of us consistently. Nevertheless, we thought we could cook up a scheme for outdoing him. We proposed a chess tournament in which all of the games were to start at six o'clock in the morning. Ostensibly this was to avoid conflict with our classes. But in fact we knew that Dougal had never gotten up as early as six o'clock in his life, so we outvoted him and put a provision in the tournament rules that said any participant who was not at the table and ready to play six o'clock a.m. would forfeit the game. He squawked like a game rooster at this rule, but, as I said, we outvoted him. He either had to accept it or withdraw from the tournament. He was too fond of beating us to withdraw.

The tournament went pretty much as we had thought it would. Dougal slept through most his scheduled matches and we enforced the forfeits. Once when he did get up in time, he as so groggy he lost the game, and I think that hurt his feelings worse than the forfeits. As the loser of the tournament, Dougal had to take us all out to a steak dinner. We enjoyed it. He didn't.

But I didn't intend to tell you about Dougal's academic career so much as about what happened to him back in Kiowa during the summer following his sophomore year. Old Spottswood had had another good year in the cotton business, and he had celebrated it by buying a new Studebaker touring car. It was as long as from here to yonder and had wheels four feet high. The boys who hung out around the drug-store said it would make seventy-five miles an hour.

Dougal took it over as if it belonged to him. This was possible because old Spottswood was gone from home a great deal and his wife was an easygoing person who never had been able to do much about controlling Dougal or any of her other children. Dougal drove the new car all over creation and covered the distance in record time. In those days a good road in Kiowa County was one in which there wasn't any danger of getting stuck in a mud hole or a sand bed. Such hazards as rocks, ruts, sharp turns, fallen tree limbs, and dead armadillos were ignored. A good driver was supposed to be able to dodge them.

This summer turned out to be Dougal's turn to try to tame Babe O'Hara. She had disposed of me and most of the other local yokels back in high school days. I don't know that she was especially attracted to Dougal, but she did like that new Studebaker. According to some of the bragging which Dougal did later, he had a date with the Babe every night for two months straight.

Usually they went to the picture show and then drove out the Post Oak City road and parked. The Babe was good at that sort of thing. I discovered that as far back as the eighth grade, and I'm sure she had improved a lot since then. I don't know how the affair would have ended if it hadn't been for a bad accident one night.

Both parties were partly at fault. Dougal was undoubtedly driving too fast as he practically always was, and just as undoubtedly he didn't have his mind on his driving. There was good reason for this. When the Babe rode in a car with a boy she sat sideways, facing the boy and with her feet up in the seat under her bottom. This posture resulted in considerable exposure of her lower parts. Dougal, I'm sure, was making the most of the view. The car hit a larger than average bump and the door which the Babe was leaning against flew open. The Babe was roughly deposited in the roadside ditch. It would have been funny if she hadn't been so badly hurt. Her right leg was broken above the knee and her hips were mangled to the point that she didn't appear in a bathing suit for the next two summers.

Old Spottswood was too stingy to spend good money on automobile liability insurance, so he had to pay all of the Babe's medical expenses. In fairness to him, however, I should point out that almost nobody had automobile insurance of any sort in those times — not in Kiowa, Texas at least.

This should have ended Dougal's wild summer but it didn't. It did end his affair with Babe O'Hara. She didn't have any more use for the big Studebaker, not to mention Dougal. Dougal pined for a few days and then revived. As soon as old Spottswood was out of town again, his son got the big car out again.

It was never clear just where he had been or where he was going, but on his way up Duncan Street toward the Presbyterian Church, he was annoyed by a country boy in a Model T Ford who tried to pass him. Dougal disliked for anybody to pass him when he was driving, but he was particularly resentful of this bumpkin in a beat-down whoopee. When the Ford was alongside of him, Dougal speeded up and wouldn't let it pass. The two cars raced up the narrow street toward the intersection at the church corner. There they were confronted by a stop sign, but they were going too fast to stop.

Unfortunately another car was entering the intersection from the right just at that moment. Dougal tried to dodge it, but he didn't have enough room to maneuver. He banged into a telephone pole, snapped it off at ground level, and sheared off the right third of the Studebaker. By grace of the fates he wasn't hurt — that is, not beyond being scared half to death. He cleared the wreckage and started running. I don't think the direction he took mattered to him at the time. But gradually he slowed down, and his mind began to work in some degree. The big need, of course, was to get out of town before old Spottswood returned. It wasn't too hard to get out of Kiowa, but Dougal wanted to get a long way out. The thing to do was to catch the west bound train at 4:20 p.m.

Dougal went through his pockets and found 35¢. He thought further and headed for Brown's Drug-store. He came in puffing and blowing.

"Listen, Cary," he said, "you've got to cash a check for me."

"We frequently cash checks for our customers," I said, "if they have a good credit rating."

"My dad has the best credit rating in town," he said.

"Is the check going to be drawn on him? " I asked.

"Yes, of course," he said.

"Go ahead," I said and handed him a pad of blank checks.

He made out one for $150 and signed it "S. McFrey by D. McFrey." I went back to the safe and got the money for him.

He didn't even count it, he just started running down Depot Street to catch the train.

I don't know where he went. I don't think he ever told anybody.

A day or two later the check I had cashed for him came back from the bank marked "Signature unauthorized." Mr. Brown hit the ceiling and threatened to fire me for my part in the transaction. He probably would have if old Spottswood hadn't come in that afternoon and paid off the check in cash money. He was saving his good name in spite of his prodigal son.

And in good traditional fashion, the prodigal son returned. It was three or four weeks after he had left and those had obviously been hard weeks for Dougal.

He was still wearing the same clothes he had on when he left and they were ragged and dirty beyond belief. He looked as bad as any tramp I have ever seen. He may have tried to get a job somewhere, but it was clear that he hadn't succeeded. Or if he had gotten one, he hadn't been able to keep it very long. He looked like No. 3 on the list of the Ten Saddest Cases.

I don't know what sort of reception he got at his home, but evidently he worked out some sort of deal with his father. The next time we saw him he was bathed, shaved, and dressed in respectable clothes. In fact, he was pretty nearly the same Dougal he had been before the catastrophe at the church corner.

But there was a difference. The next Monday morning he appeared in work clothes with the gang that was paving the courthouse square. He was slinging a sledgehammer to knock out the forms from some concrete that had been poured the week before. It was a sight worth seeing—Dougal McFrey engaged in manual labor. People who knew him stopped and stared. Hody Sparks, who was planning a career as a news photographer, took several pictures of him in action. Dougal grinned and bore it.

But the Reformation didn't last. Dougal wasn't necessarily lazy. He had played a right good game at left tackle on the K.H.S. football team. But he couldn't get up in the morning to get to work on time. When he had been late three mornings out of five, the boss fired him.

It was now about the middle of September and time for us to go back to the University, but old Spottswood put his foot down solidly and refused to pay for any more alleged higher education for Dougal. Instead, he sent him down to Hasse to buy cotton.

Hasse wasn't much more than a wide place in the road. It had two stores, a filling station, a cotton gin, and six houses. Dougal was stuck down there with very little to do and no car to get away in. He just couldn't stand it. All of a sudden he simply disappeared. Nobody knew where. He went out of our lives like a kerosene lantern in a tornado.

But when we came home for the Christmas recess, there was Dougal all dressed up and looking relatively prosperous. He told us he was in "industrial banking" in San Antonio. We learned later that this meant he had a job in a loan-shark outfit, a racket where poor Negroes and Mexicans and a few Anglos borrowed $10 and paid back 50¢ a week for the rest of their lives without ever reducing the principle of their debt.

But this was not the end of Dougal's business career, by any means. He saved a few thousand dollars and went out to Pecos, Texas, where they were beginning to grow cotton with irrigation water from a new dam on the Pecos River. They used natural gas, of which there was a big supply in the area, to pump the water and fuel the farm machinery.

Dougal persuaded one of the banks in the town of Pecos to finance him, and he went into cotton-buying in a big way. He was good at it, and made a lot of money. He married a very nice girl whom he had met out there, and they started a family.

Unfortunately in about twenty years the supply of natural gas ran out and irrigated farming in the area died out. But by that time old Spottswood had accommodatingly died of a heart attack, and Dougal came back to Kiowa and took over all of the family businesses.

As of now he is a solid citizen of the town and a pillar of all good works in the community.

The moral of this story: Never despair of your bratty offspring.